MAGIC
MOVIE
MOMENTS

MAGIC
MOVIE
MOMENTS

**BOB ADELMAN AND
MICHAEL RAND
COMMENTARY BY
GEORGE PERRY
INTRODUCTION BY
TERRY GILLIAM**

A BOB ADELMAN BOOK

VIKING STUDIO

Acknowledgments

Magic Movie Moments started with a still photographer's perception that in certain motion pictures there are frames that are riveting photographs. To flesh out that notion required the herculean efforts of Michael Rand, photography's third eye. He sifted through thousands of images and found 150 or so very diverse ones that he inventively orchestrated to work together. George Perry brought his encyclopedic knowledge, his love of films and anecdotes, and his felicity for lively expression to illuminate every one of the moments. Adam Brown refined and enhanced every page with his discriminating taste and judgment, building on an earlier handsome presentation by Ian Denning. We are grateful to Mary Corliss and Terry Geesken from the Museum of Modern Art for sharing their intricate knowledge of film and for helping us to find the right moments. Christopher Sweet instantly saw what we were trying to do and was amazingly supportive, generously lending his refined visual sense to the book as well as his publishing smarts. We are fortunate that Mary Beth Brewer brought her many talents to all phases of the book's creation, from picture research to editorial clarity.
Bob Adelman

A Bob Adelman Book

Editor: Mary Beth Brewer
Art Director: Michael Rand
Design: B+B

VIKING STUDIO
Published by the Penguin Group
Penguin Putnam Inc., 375 Hudson Street,
New York, New York 10014, U.S.A.
Penguin Books Ltd, 27 Wrights Lane,
London W8 5TZ, England
Penguin Books Australia Ltd, Ringwood,
Victoria, Australia
Penguin Books Canada Ltd, 10 Alcorn Avenue,
Toronto, Ontario, Canada M4V 3B2
Penguin Books (N.Z.) Ltd,
182-190 Wairau Road, Aukland 10, New Zealand

Penguin Books Ltd, Registered Offices:
Harmondsworth, Middlesex, England

First published in 2000 by Viking Studio,
a member of Penguin Putnam Inc.

10 9 8 7 6 5 4 3 2 1

CIP data available
ISBN 0-670-88932-6

Printed in Hong Kong
Set in England

Frontispiece: Intolerance, 1916.
Directed by D. W. Griffith.

Contents

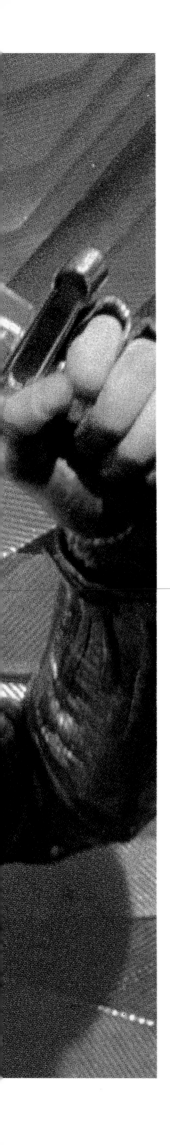

Introduction

Terry Gilliam

For directors magic moments are often accidental and unplanned and become apparent only after the finished film has had a response from the audience. Be suspicious when magic moments are deliberately created; they can often fail. Filmmaking is actually a far more arbitrary process than is generally realized, one of the reasons it is so exciting. Sadly we are living in an age of the simulacra: Everything seems to be a copy of what has gone before. That is the difficulty of making a movie now. How do you manage to be new and original? Most modern filmmakers have been raised in film schools where they endlessly go over the films of the past. Their minds are filled with so much that their works turn out to be an assembly of all their favorite moments. Their difficulty is that they want to be original but know too much.

Tarantino was a nice surprise. It was not that he ignored the past but that he used it and transformed it. Actually, Pulp Fiction was not as good as people thought it was. It is a mixed bag of goodies. It pretends to show a real, cool world, but it is a world that exists only in cinema. But we bought it. Quentin is very talented, and a lot of critics in America missed out on recognizing the brilliance of Reservoir Dogs, so they zoomed in on Pulp Fiction instead. It was like the second coming.

A director can try too hard. Stanley Kubrick became less good as he went on because of his obsessiveness. Unable to choose from five locations for a restaurant scene, he would shoot the same sequence in all of them. My own experience has often shown me you have to steel yourself and say, Now's the day—I have got to do it. Everybody can then focus on that moment. If you go back to it a second time it no longer has the same intensity.

The pages in this book remind me of so much. Potemkin fits the age when I was discovering foreign movies at college. Eisenstein used imagery in a way that was different from western films. I remember watching amazed, and came out of the theater changed, realizing that you could say all these important things. It was my first real turning point.

In Lawrence of Arabia the location cinematography is marvelous, and it is beautifully edited. When you look at the interiors you see

Brazil, 1985. Directed by Terry Gilliam.

terrible makeup and poor lighting. You cannot separate the film from the Maurice Jarre score, which eventually becomes unendurable. Peter O'Toole used to laugh about the fact that they were wearing frocks all the time. "Florence of Arabia" he called it. He had a nose job to play the part, and sadly he had had a great nose before. Neither he nor Omar Sharif could top that film.

Steve McQueen was magical in The Great Escape, an otherwise unremarkable film. There is an indefinable quality nobody seems to understand that makes certain actors a magnet for our attention. McQueen seems authentic, the real thing. There is an integrity there that you are not supposed to be able to fake. In fact, a lot of actors fake it all the time.

Apocalypse Now was everything that was awful and wonderful about the Vietnam War. As the colonel, Duvall was never better. His men use artificial means to get high, but this man is natural, the stuff is coursing through every fiber of his body. It belongs to the period when I left the States for England because of America's involvement. I was unable to deal with the madness that was going on in the States. When I saw Duvall's scene I thought this was it, they have finally reduced the war to one character who shows everything that has gone wrong with it. The film could have been just this one scene, and it would have summed up the entire mess.

When it comes to romance, the images hang in the air. You want real life to be like that and it never is. We go through life hoping to live one of those moments, almost as if there is a camera watching us. Clark Gable carrying Scarlet up the stairs is doing what we are supposed to do as men, taking control, taking the woman, who is a feisty little fighter, and winning her.

The French New Wave was my magic moment. Suddenly seeing movies like Breathless became a whole new way of looking. In Jules and Jim you could have the bittersweet comedy, and even if people died it wasn't awful. It was what life should be about, living for the moment and dying for the moment. I realized that there was a whole world waiting for me if I could get out of America then and escape from the Hollywood rules of what you could say on film. The French broke those rules, and Jules and Jim still holds up. Buñuel also did it. He made films about moments. He would take all our conventions and push our noses in them.

I started on Fellini with La Dolce Vita. I am fascinated by Anita Ekberg's iconic pose in the fountain. It triggers many things for me, seeing this pretentious, loopy woman who is totally monumental. And next to her Ursula Andress, Ursula rising, Venus with a shell, a dangerous babe.

Polanski was like Lang, Stroheim, Wilder, and Lubitsch, bringing a European sensibility to Hollywood. The way all those various characters related to each other in Chinatown was not how it was done in American films. What is The Maltese Falcon about? It is like Chinatown in that I can't get my fingers on what it is. It does not hold up if you start to analyze it, yet it seems utterly true and real. You want to believe it. It's

Lawrence of Arabia, 1962. David Lean.

La Dolce Vita, 1960. Frederico Fellini.

great, even if Bogie does send his babe up the river. There is a wartime morality about it, the stand-by-your-buddy-no-matter-what factor.

Clint Eastwood is the smartest guy in Hollywood because he uses his power to make interesting films. One for them, one for me. Nobody else has been as canny. Dirty Harry drove a lot of people crazy because it is so politically incorrect. I give him a lot of points for that. I don't have to agree with him, but I like the way he confronts the issues. By then we had given up on the idea of the lone hero. But he is a cop. You ought to compare it with High Noon. They are mirror images of the same thing. In many ways Dirty Harry was ahead of its time. I did not have a problem with it; it is the old western genre being put to use here, brought up to date. Note Play Misty for Me on the theater marquee. A director's indulgence. I did that in The Fisher King. If you look behind Jeff Bridges in the video shop the posters are all of my films. You have got to take every possible moment to advertise.

Bonnie and Clyde captures the age more than Easy Rider, which was specific. Bonnie and Clyde does it more abstractedly. Two people in love are going against society, making bank robbery look fun, and then the bloody death, straight out of Kurosawa country. I like magic moments like this because they are neither good nor bad.

I remember riding my bicycle home after watching Psycho, down Van Nuys Boulevard in a state of shock. Nobody had taken a famous actress and bumped her off in the first third of the film. It is so bold and outrageous and wonderful and shows the utter perverseness of Hitchcock. You know that he is going to be doing things with us, playing with us the way no one else could. You go in, waiting to be fiddled with in the dark in a grand way. For me the big moment in the shower scene is that blurred silhouette against the curtain. Very little information is given, but your mind is crazed.

Psycho, 1960. Alfred Hitchcock.

What is great about The Exorcist image is that it implies everything and gives away nothing. I remember mostly the sound from that film, when you get a hard cut and a sudden loud noise. Three or four times the audience is jolted by something that turns out to be innocuous. But they are being so softened up that the terror of seeing what will happen next in the bedroom becomes unbearable.

In the 1960s I discovered Keaton and realized that he was the real master, not Chaplin. He had that extraordinary precision, like Fred Astaire. And like Jackie Chan he did all his own stunts. At no point does he ask for my sympathy or do anything cute to win me over. Just the stone face. He was breathtakingly original and a great genius.

With the Marx Brothers the shock was learning that these anarchic films came from months on the road perfecting the jokes. True anarchy, the spirit of anarchy, is needed on the screen and this is it. But it only comes about with precision and control. Nobody else then was doing absurdist humor. We tried with Python.

Ealing comedies were one of the reasons I emigrated to England. It was different humor to that in the States, and it sucked me over there. It was so much more sophisticated and witty than anything being done in America. So I went to England and lowered the tone.

Stand by Your Pianos

◀ In France at the close of World War I, Busby Berkeley taught General Pershing's doughboys to drill by numbers without shouted commands, a parade-ground sensation that made the brass ecstatic. His skills were snapped up by Broadway and then Hollywood, where his geometrical, kaleidoscopic formations of beautiful girls defined the choreography of a succession of glitzy, mindless Warner musicals. In this number even the pianos twirled and waltzed to The Words Are in My Heart. How? Under each one was a man in black who knew what to do. Everybody in the thirties copied Berkeley's eye-catching precision, from the Rockettes at Radio City to the stormtroopers of the Nuremberg rallies.
Gold Diggers of 1935, 1935.
Director: Busby Berkeley.
Starring: Dick Powell, Gloria Stuart, Adolphe Menjou, Glenda Farrell.

Facing the Music

◄ Ginger Rogers is about to be fired from her job as a dance instructor because her pupil Fred Astaire is so inept, but then he whisks her into the sublime Pick Yourself Up number in the best of their ten romantic comedies with music. Helping was a classic score by Jerome Kern, which also included A Fine Romance and The Way You Look Tonight. Astaire had classier, more accomplished partners than Rogers, and in private life they were not close friends. Yet on screen she was absolutely right for him, a great professional dancer who never allowed her style to overshadow his, while he in turn made sure she always looked terrific. Astaire was the greatest of screen dancers, but Balanchine went further, saying that he was the greatest dancer he had ever seen.
Swing Time, 1936.
Director: George Stevens.
Starring: Fred Astaire, Ginger Rogers, Victor Moore, Helen Broderick, Eric Blore.

Strutting His Stuff

▲ John Travolta as Tony Manero, Brooklyn's king of the disco floor, takes center stage in the role that made him an overnight cult hero. As he hits the insistent beat, his partner (Karen Lynn Gorney) is rendered invisible. The Saturday night disco serves as the same kind of escape hatch from dreary everyday routine as the dance floors in the movies from the thirties featuring Fred and Ginger. Tony wants out of Brooklyn and his hardware-store day job and has Manhattan's neon glow in his sights. The film evolved from a cover story in New York Magazine by Nik Cohn, Tribal Rites of the New Saturday Night, which Norman Wexler neatly fictionalized for the screen.
Saturday Night Fever, 1977.
Director: John Badham.
Starring: John Travolta, Karen Lynn Gorney, Barry Miller, Donna Pescow.

Not in Kansas Anymore?

▲ The Scarecrow (Ray Bolger), The Tin Man (Jack Haley), Dorothy (Judy Garland) with her dog Toto, and the Cowardly Lion (Bert Lahr) trip along the Yellow Brick Road on the last leg of their journey to the Emerald City where they hope the Wizard will grant their dearest wishes. Allegedly, through endless television screenings more people have seen this picture than any other. So potent is the film's magic that it transcends the stories of L. Frank Baum on which it is based. The breathtaking special effects and spectacular use of Technicolor broke new ground, but costumes and makeup caused agonies, even hospitalization for the actors. Having seen the glitzy Emerald City, why should Dorothy want to go back to Kansas? Because "there's no place like home" was the universal message.

The Wizard of Oz, 1939.
Directors: Victor Fleming, King Vidor.
Starring: Judy Garland, Ray Bolger, Bert Lahr, Jack Haley, Billie Burke, Margaret Hamilton.

The Wizard of Oz 1939

The Room's Spinning

◄ When Fred Astaire danced lovestruck around the room he did it literally, encompassing the walls and ceiling as well as the floor in the number You're All the World to Me, the highpoint of one of his lesser films for the MGM producer Arthur Freed. Today the special effects would be easy, achievable through blue-screen and computer-generated imagery for a mere couple million dollars or so. In those naive days half a century ago they simply bolted the camera to the floor of the set, which was built as a rotating cube and set in motion at appropriate moments. The result, pure cinema magic.

Royal Wedding, 1951.
Director: Stanley Donen.
Starring: Fred Astaire, Jane Powell, Peter Lawford, Sarah Churchill.

Royal Wedding 1951

C'mon Everybody, Let's Rock

▲ Elvis Presley may have been the greatest entertainer of the twentieth century, certainly the king of rock 'n' roll, but almost without exception his 33 movies from 1956 to 1969, while usually fulfilling box-office expectations, are anodyne duds. The best one came early in his film career and works because his character is not exactly Mr. Nice Guy. Instead he is an arrogant, prickly rocker whose short-fused temper lands him in the Big House, where he learns improved guitar technique. Back in the world and becoming famous, he uses his prison experience as the basis for this production number to entertain the TV millions. Elvis choreographed it himself, and his hip-swiveling charisma never came across better.

Jailhouse Rock, 1957.
Director: Richard Thorpe.
Starring: Elvis Presley, Judy Tyler, Mickey Shaughnessy.

Jailhouse Rock 1957

Come On with the Rain

▶ Gene Kelly was coming down with the flu and carried on even though he was fighting a raging temperature. The so-called rain was half-water, half-milk so the Technicolor camera could see it. Consequently, after three days shooting the set stank to high heaven and Kelly's suit shrank. Should we care? Hardly. Because Kelly, ever the pro, brilliantly conveys that the hero is suddenly aware that he's in love, letting us in on one of the most joyous musical numbers ever filmed, in perhaps the best movie Hollywood ever made about Hollywood.
Singin' in the Rain, 1952.
Directors: Gene Kelly, Stanley Donen.
Starring: Gene Kelly, Donald O'Connor, Debbie Reynolds.

Making a Splash

▲ "I'm gonna wash that man right out of my hair," trills Mitzi Gaynor as Ensign Nellie Forbush in the screen version of the eternal Rodgers and Hammerstein stage hit. Mary Martin created the role on stage, but amazingly Joshua Logan wanted Elizabeth Taylor for the role. She considered it, but flubbed a singing tryout in front of Rodgers. Doris Day also clammed up. Gaynor was to be the only principal who sang with her own voice. Rossano Brazzi ("that man"), as the French planter caught up in the war, was dubbed by Giorgio Tozzi. Even Juanita Hall, the sole survivor from Broadway, had her singing dubbed for the film. Critically it was not a success, and even the director disowned the garish color processing, but it made more money than all Logan's other stage and film productions put together.
South Pacific, 1958.
Director: Joshua Logan.
Starring: Rossano Brazzi, Mitzi Gaynor, John Kerr, Ray Walston.

The Singing Nun

▲ The enduring screen image of the rosy-cheeked
Julie Andrews is the swooping helicopter shot of
her in a high Alpine meadow rotating in her dirndl
skirt and singing at full lung power "The hills are
alive with the sound of music." The story of the
postulant who leaves the nunnery to become
a governess to a singing family, eventually helping
them all to flee from the Nazis who have seized
Austria, was not Rodgers and Hammerstein's
most inspired stage work, yet it became the most
successful musical ever filmed, with some
devotees returning to see it more than a hundred
times. Schmaltz has never been better than this.
The Sound of Music, 1965.
Director: Robert Wise.
*Starring: Julie Andrews, Christopher Plummer,
Eleanor Parker.*

Dancing up
a Storm

▶ Yul Brynner had played the Siamese king so
many times in Rodgers and Hammerstein's hit on
Broadway that he more or less defined the role,
eclipsing Rex Harrison's earlier portrayal in a
nonmusical version of Margaret Landon's
biography of Anna Leonowens. The filmmakers'
inspiration was to cast Deborah Kerr as the
Victorian governess who has sailed from England
to look after the king's many children. Historical
revisionists now tell us that the real Anna was
a bit of a phony, neither as upper-class as she
pretended to be nor as close to the king as her
memoirs suggest. Worse, modern Thailand
cordially detests the representation of their
monarch as a barbarian who waltzed barefoot.
The King and I, 1956.
Director: Walter Lang.
Starring: Yul Brynner, Deborah Kerr, Rita Moreno.

A Plague on Both Your Houses

▶ The Sharks and the Jets take control of their streets in the riveting opening sequence shot on location in New York's Hell's Kitchen district in the otherwise studiobound production of the 1957 Stephen Sondheim-Leonard Bernstein Broadway musical. The choreographer, Jerome Robbins, adapted his style from stage to pavement, his dancers weaving past parked cars in an electric surge of acrobatic movement. The Romeo and Juliet theme transferred well to a Manhattan setting, but Natalie Wood (her singing dubbed by Marin Nixon) was an uncertain heroine and Richard Beymer a pretty but bloodless hero. Both were overshadowed by the second leads, George Chakiris and Rita Moreno. But with ten Oscars, who can complain?
West Side Story, 1961.
Director: Robert Wise.
Starring: Natalie Wood, Richard Beymer, Russ Tamblyn, Rita Moreno, George Chakiris.

West Side Story 1961

I Say, Will You Get a Move On?

▲ Julie Andrews made the Lerner-Loewe Broadway musical based on George Bernard Shaw's Pygmalion her own, and that she failed to land the film role was a huge mystery. One explanation is that the testy Rex Harrison was so jealous of her nightly standing ovations that he refused to do the movie with her. Cary Grant actually had been offered his part and turned it down. Audrey Hepburn looked wonderful, but was unconvincing in the early scenes as the Cockney Eliza before Professor Higgins worked on her. Nor was her singing up to the role, and she was dubbed by the reliable Marni Nixon. Cecil Beaton's costumes, evoking the fashions of 1912, were legendary, and the Ascot moment when Eliza's new ladylike demeanor falters as she yells to a horse to move its "bleedin' ass" is a memorable highpoint. When it was Oscar time the best actress award went to Julie Andrews — for Mary Poppins. Audrey Hepburn was not even nominated.
My Fair Lady, 1964.
Director: George Cukor.
Starring: Rex Harrison, Audrey Hepburn, Stanley Holloway, Wilfrid Hyde-White.

Whatever Happened to Broadway?

▶ The long-limbed Cyd Charisse and Fred Astaire perform the Girl Hunt Ballet, a satirical dance sequence modeled on Mickey Spillane-style pulp fiction in this great backstage musical. Much of it seems like a roman-a-clef. Fred Astaire plays a Hollywood star who feels he's over the hill and can't cut it on Broadway, and, worse, thinks that Charisse might be too tall to be his partner. The writers of the show in the film, played by Nanette Fabray and Oscar Levant, parallel Betty Comden and Adolph Green, who were the writers of the screenplay. The towering theatrical figure played by Jack Buchanan, whose artistic pretensions nearly threaten the project, is said by some to be a loose spoof of Orson Welles. It was not a joyous production: Buchanan was in agony from dental problems, Astaire's wife died during shooting, Levant was recovering from a heart attack, and Fabray suffered a bad leg cut. To paraphrase: That's Entertainment.
The Band Wagon, 1953.
Director: Vincente Minnelli.
Starring: Fred Astaire, Jack Buchanan, Cyd Charisse.

In the Cannon's Mouth

▶ Early in the history of film, D. W. Griffith's Civil War epic, running three hours to audiences more accustomed to two-reelers, provided scores of extraordinary cinematic images. Battlefield scenes were created with the cinematographer Billy Bitzer to echo the feeling of Matthew Brady's contemporary photographs of the conflict.

In this moment of high drama, Henry B. Walthall, playing a brave Southerner, rams the Confederate flag down the barrel of a Union cannon. Griffith, having used a creaky, bigoted novel, The Clansman, as his source, came under fierce criticism for the film's racist stance, and screenings of this masterpiece usually have to be accompanied by an explanatory text.

The Birth of a Nation, 1915.
Director: D. W. Griffith.
Starring: Lillian Gish, Mae Marsh,
Henry B. Walthall.

The Birth of a Nation 1915

Film Revolution

◀ Is this the most famous sequence in the history of movies? The Tsarist massacre on the Odessa steps, following the 1905 sailors' mutiny on the Battleship Potemkin, has been endlessly analyzed and imitated. Eisenstein, only twenty-seven when he made his stirring historical study, formulated a theory of editing with rapid cuts. This "montage" technique became a fundamental element of the grammar of film. Scenes of civilians shot by the indiscriminate firing of the Tsar's troops shocked audiences, particularly when a young mother is cut down and a baby carriage hurtles down the steps. In Britain the film was banned as Communist propaganda. In Russia Stalin suppressed it because mutiny in the Soviet armed forces was not to be encouraged.

Potemkin, 1925.
Director: Sergei Eisenstein.
Starring: Alexander Antonov, Vladimir Barsky, Grigori Alexandrov.

Potemkin 1925

The Turning Point

▲ Renoir's sensitive masterpiece examines the changes to society wrought by war. After receiving serious wounds in action, an aristocratic German air ace (Erich von Stroheim, center) is relegated to running a prison camp for officers in a fortified castle. He greets two transferred Frenchmen, a fellow aristocrat (Pierre Fresnay, center right) and a former mechanic (Jean Gabin, right) who has been awarded a commission. The two elitists are cut from the same cloth and lament the passing of an age that understood their values. The exigencies of war will terminate their accord, but it is the working-class man who has the resolution to survive. As Pauline Kael observes, to describe this great film as an escape story is like saying that Oedipus Rex is a detective story. In World War II the Nazis suppressed it.

La Grande Illusion, 1937.
Director: Jean Renoir.
Starring: Jean Gabin, Pierre Fresnay,
Erich von Stroheim, Marcel Dalio.

Futile Gesture

▶ One of Alec Guinness's greatest screen roles was as Colonel Nicholson, the indomitable commander of a British regiment in Japanese captivity after the surrender of Burma in 1942. Engaged in a battle of wills with the camp commandant (Sessue Hayakawa) he holds to the Geneva Convention and refuses to allow his officers to undergo manual labor. In spite of prolonged spells in the sweat box he wins his point. The construction of a rail bridge becomes a project to keep up his men's morale, but he becomes obsessed with its completion, forgetting that it will serve as an enemy supply route.

The Bridge on the River Kwai, 1957.
Director: David Lean.
Starring: Alec Guinness, Sessue Hayakawa,
William Holden, James Donald.

Desert Fury

▶ Lawrence (Peter O'Toole) exults in his triumph after leading a destructive attack on an enemy train on the Hejaz desert railroad. O'Toole, then a little-known actor, stood nearly a foot taller than the real T. E. Lawrence, and imposed his extraordinary presence on every frame of David Lean's long film. At the same time he conveyed distance, a mystic remoteness from his fellows that was entirely in keeping with the enigmatic hero he was playing. That Lawrence was an inspirational figure to the Arabs in the Middle East during World War I is not in doubt, but to this day his real achievement is a matter of debate. Robert Bolt's screenplay, the wondrous location cinematography by the legendary Freddie Young, a supporting cast of substantial British and American names, the impressive western debut of the Egyptian Omar Sharif, and, especially, Lean's measured direction in which a great adventure becomes a study in psychology — contribute to a significant film. After mutilations by its distributor, Lawrence of Arabia was happily restored to its original length shortly before the director died.

Lawrence of Arabia, 1962.
Director: David Lean.
Starring: Peter O'Toole, Alec Guinness, Anthony Quinn, Jack Hawkins, Jose Ferrer, Claude Rains, Arthur Kennedy, Omar Sharif.

Lawrence of Arabia 1962

Uneasy Rider

◀ Steve McQueen played Hilts, "The Cooler King," in the archetypal prisoner-of-war escape film and managed to steal the show from an ensemble cast. An enthusiast for hard traveling, he did much of the hairy riding himself, although the famous leap in which he attempted to ride a stolen German bike over a fence at the Swiss border was more likely to have been made by his motorcycle mentor, Bud Ekins. The wartime BMW he rides was really a heavily disguised Triumph TTS Special 650. When not escaping, McQueen's character did time in solitary, endlessly bouncing a baseball against a wall into his mitt. There was a suppressed air of anger about him that set him apart from the others, to the point that the director threatened to fire him, yet it perfectly fitted the role he played. McQueen died young, at fifty, from a heart attack while undergoing chest cancer surgery, his vital screen presence prematurely snuffed out.
The Great Escape, 1963.
Director: John Sturges.
Starring: Steve McQueen, James Garner, Richard Attenborough.

Our Blood and His Guts

▶ George S. Patton was the fiercest, most ornery American general of World War II, a formidable fighter who argued with his superiors, angered his equals, shocked his allies, and terrified his men. What he did to the enemy was the stuff of legend. George C. Scott, playing him on film, went for it as the part of a lifetime and outshone the real Patton in flamboyant belligerence. The film begins with a stirring six-minute pep talk to the audience in front of a huge stars-and-stripes. Scott, as if a part of Patton's cantankerousness had entered his soul, compounded his achievement by refusing to accept the Oscar awarded to him as Best Actor.
Patton, 1970.
Director: Franklin J. Schaffner.
Starring: George C. Scott, Karl Malden, Michael Bates.

Surf's Up, Colonel

▲ "I love the smell of napalm in the morning," exclaims Lt. Col. Kilgore (Robert Duvall) as his gunships fly in with stereo speakers pumping out Ride of the Valkyries and proceed to blast a Vietnamese coastal village off the map. Mission accomplished, the colonel encourages some of his boys to test the surf, having brought along a few boards. Coppola's epic, claiming inspiration from Joseph Conrad's Heart of Darkness, is essentially a focus on madness, with a quest for another insane colonel (Marlon Brando) who has gone to ground with an army of AWOL followers on the Cambodian border. Brando was paid a million dollars for a few incoherent minutes, but in this memorable scene Duvall outclasses him.
Apocalypse Now, 1979.
Director: Francis Ford Coppola.
Starring: Marlon Brando, Robert Duvall, Martin Sheen, Frederic Forrest.

God for England

▼ "Once more unto the breach," cries Laurence Olivier as Shakespeare's Plantagenet king preparing his troops for battle against the French at Harfleur. The historical epic had many resonances for the British, with the D-Day landings, the invasion of Fortress Europe, and the airborne assault on Arnhem all real-life events within the ambit of the film's release. Its heady patriotism stirred souls. When Kenneth Branagh attempted the same role 45 years later he was able to make Henry a darker, less noble warmonger. Olivier masterminded an austerity production in which armor was made from papier-mache, chain mail from wool sprayed with aluminum paint, and swords from carved wood. The Agincourt battle scenes had to be filmed in neutral Ireland, away from German air attacks and with a plentiful supply of extras from the Irish army available for action.
Henry V, 1944.
Director: Laurence Olivier.
Starring: Laurence Olivier, Robert Newton, Leslie Banks, Renee Asherson, Esmond Knight.

Henry V 1944

Freedom for Scotland

▶ A new national identity was forged for Scotland by an Australian actor who spent the first 12 years of his life in the United States. Mel Gibson evoked a Scottish hero from about 1300 who led his people against the English. Not much is really known about William Wallace beyond his legendary feat of uniting the clans, which is narrated in an old epic poem. Historical fact rarely stands in the way of dedicated filmmakers, and Gibson's film, dubbed Mad Mac by some, made astonishing leaps into fiction. The English come out badly, and many Scots believe that even if the story isn't strictly true the spirit of Braveheart most surely is. The other trend the film fostered is the face-painting with national flags by soccer fans at big matches.
Braveheart, 1995.
Director: Mel Gibson.
Starring: Mel Gibson, Sophie Marceau, Patrick McGoohan.

The Breakfast Club

▶ The moment James Cagney, annoyed by a floosie (Mae Clarke) after a dud night, thrust half a grapefruit into her face made the tiny, mercurial actor playing a cocky gangster a true star. Clarke later claimed that Cagney and the director William Wellman had tricked her and that she was merely meant to be shouted at, so the one-take reaction caught by the camera—shock, surprise, and humiliation—is genuine. If so, it did her career no harm, although women's organizations of the day made loud protests over the scene and also those that involved Jean Harlow as a call girl with a yen for violent customers. It endures as one of the best films of the Prohibition era.

The Public Enemy, 1931.
Director: William A Wellman.
Starring: James Cagney, Jean Harlow,
Eddie Woods, Joan Blondell.

Farewell My Love

▶ Garbo's role as Dumas's La Dame Aux Camelias was perhaps the apogee of her career. A woman with a past, she leaves the baron who has been keeping her for a young man, Robert Taylor, then twenty-five. Unlike the rest of Paris, he has no idea that she is a courtesan, and to spare his shame she gives him up, although of course she doesn't mean it. In the famous ending, when she is dying of tuberculosis, they are reunited. Never did Hollywood deliver a more romantic deathbed scene.
Camille, 1937.
Director: George Cukor.
Starring: Greta Garbo, Robert Taylor, Lionel Barrymore.

Love on the Brink

▶ Brando as Stanley, oozing sensuality in the adaptation of Tennessee Williams's drama, has had his slobbish New Orleans easy-loving style disrupted by the arrival of his wife's neurotic sister, Blanche. In this key moment he has begged his pregnant wife, Stella (Kim Hunter), to forgive him for his drunken trashing of their shabby apartment, and he presses his head against her body to hear the heartbeat of their unborn child.
In a censorial mood, Hollywood sheared the scene, and it was not until the 1993 restoration that its subtlety was revealed.
A Streetcar Named Desire, 1951.
Director: Elia Kazan.
Starring: Vivien Leigh, Marlon Brando, Kim Hunter, Karl Malden.

Mild Interest at First Sight

▶ Woody Allen's study in insecurity seems intensely personal. That he and Diane Keaton were partners at the time shows in the close-knit interplay of their respective characters, he a neurotic New York comedy writer, she a nervous aspiring singer from the Midwest with a gauche dress sense that would eventually become ultimate chic. Their early encounters are tense, introspective, and hilarious as they fumble toward a relationship, which will be doomed by jealousy and self-doubt. It is Woody's key work, and behind the laughs the pain shows through.
Annie Hall, 1977.
Director: Woody Allen.
Starring: Woody Allen, Diane Keaton, Tony Roberts, Carol Kane.

Camille 1937

A Streetcar Named Desire 1951

Annie Hall 1977

Heartache on the Moors

◀ Heathcliff is an abandoned child who has grown up at Wuthering Heights inseparable from Cathy, the daughter of his benefactor. Here they sublimate their passion on a craggy moorland rock, their favorite overlook. Laurence Olivier wanted Vivien Leigh to play Cathy, and Merle Oberon would have preferred Douglas Fairbanks, Jr., as Heathcliff, but both submerged their froideur before the camera. There were other difficulties, some brought on by exposure to the rain-soaked Yorkshire moors, which were lovingly recreated in the Conejo Hills in southern California where heather and, rather surprisingly, tumbleweed were planted in huge quantities. Oberon caught a serious chill and injured an ankle, while Olivier also hobbled for much of the time with severe athlete's foot. They also suffered from William Wyler's perfectionist directing style, which their co-star David Niven had already endured on Dodsworth. The result, even if only the first half of Emily Bronte's searing novel was used, was one of the most romantic films to reach the screen, and Olivier was later to claim that Wyler taught him how to act for films.
Wuthering Heights, 1939.
Director: William Wyler.
Starring: Merle Oberon, Laurence Olivier, David Niven.

Wuthering Heights 1939

The Noble Savage

▲ Edgar Rice Burroughs, the creator of Tarzan, published the first Tarzan book in 1914, and Elmo Lincoln portrayed the character on screen in 1918. Many others have played him, but the most famous is still the former Olympic swimmer Johnny Weissmuller, who made a dozen appearances in the role. In many respects Tarzan is the ideal eco-hero, an orphan raised by animals, an innocent unsullied by civilization, with a deep concern for the protection of his natural environment. The advent of Jane (Maureen Sullivan) into his jungle world throws him into a whirl. He never actually says "me Tarzan, you Jane," but the sparse dialogue is not so very far removed. Jane in turn is happy to abandon her fiancé and remain with the primates for further adventures.
Tarzan, the Ape Man, 1932.
Director: W. S. Van Dyke.
Starring: Johnny Weissmuller, Maureen O'Sullivan, Neil Hamilton, C. Aubrey Smith.

Tarzan, the Ape Man 1932

A Foreign Affair

◀ Garbo's twenty-sixth and penultimate film was her first comedy, and "Garbo Laughs" was the famous billboard cry. In Ernst Lubitsch's film she plays a dour commissar sent by the Soviets to discipline an errant trade delegation that has succumbed to the capitalist delights of Paris, and she finds herself the target of a suave count (Melvyn Douglas) who tries to make her lighten up. In the celebrated restaurant scene she remains stone-faced when he tells joke after joke. Exasperated, he accidentally falls off his chair. She laughs uncontrollably. From then on five-year plans, tractors, and Stalin are forgotten. She becomes a pushover for satin lingerie, silk stockings, and expensive perfume. Among the screenwriters was Lubitsch's fellow expatriate, Billy Wilder.
Ninotchka, 1939.
Director: Ernst Lubitsch.
Starring: Greta Garbo, Melvyn Douglas, Ina Claire.

No Gentleman and No Lady

◀ Rhett Butler (Clark Gable) and Scarlet O'Hara (Vivien Leigh) probably deserved each other, he a Civil War profiteer and opportunist who until his conscience catches up leaves fighting to the idealists and she, headstrong, willful and defiant, even when demonstrably wrong. At left, he tries to dissuade her from leaving war-ravaged Atlanta for Tara, her ruined family estate. At right, the disillusioned husband asserts his marital rights: "This is one night you're not going to turn me out." It takes 220 minutes of the 222-minute running time for her to realize that she really has loved Rhett all the time, but by then she is too late. He has told her "Frankly, my dear, I don't give a damn." Why is the wrong word emphasized? Because then "damn" was not a word used lightly, and permission was granted on condition it was not stressed. In 60 years the power of David O. Selznick's epic version of Margaret Mitchell's best seller has survived, and modern prints have recaptured its former sumptuousness.
Gone with the Wind, 1939.
Director: Victor Fleming.
Starring: Clark Gable, Vivien Leigh, Leslie Howard, Olivia de Havilland.

You Must Remember This

◄ In that murky lighting so characteristic of Warner's during wartime a miracle took place on a Burbank soundstage. The cast is assembled at the airport for the finale of Casablanca. Ilsa (Ingrid Bergman) is about to make a choice between Rick (Humphrey Bogart), trench-coated owner of the Cafe American and Victor (Paul Henreid), the underground hero at the rear, while the police chief (Claude Rains) addresses a subordinate. Warner's great wartime weepy is often thought to be the most serendipitous movie of all time. Yet the irascible director Michael Curtiz raged so hard at the bit player (left) for fumbling his line that the three incensed leading actors walked off the set and hid for several hours until an apology came.

Casablanca, 1942.
Director: Michael Curtiz.
Starring: Humphrey Bogart, Ingrid Bergman, Claude Rains, Paul Henreid.

The Haunting Image

◄ A detective (Dana Andrews) investigating a murder in a chic Manhattan apartment falls in love with the victim (Gene Tierney), sniffing her perfume, rummaging through her closets, and staring endlessly at her portrait. One night the front door opens, and in she walks. A magnificent film noir with a haunting theme tune by David Raksin, it was a troubled production, with Darryl F. Zanuck, then head of Twentieth Century Fox, firing the director Rouben Mamoulian in mid-shoot, replacing him with the unpopular Otto Preminger. Nevertheless, Mamoulian gave it some great plot twists and urged the brilliant casting of Clifton Webb as an acerbic, sexually ambivalent columnist whose obsession matches that of Andrews.

Laura, 1944.

Director: Otto Preminger.

Starring: Dana Andrews, Gene Tierney, Clifton Webb, Vincent Price.

Laura 1944

"Fasten Your Seatbelts"

▼ Bette Davis was not the first choice to play the actress Margo Channing, perennial toast of Broadway, until the ambitious ingenue and supposed adoring fan Eve Harrington (Anne Baxter, far left) comes along to knock her off her perch. Claudette Colbert cried off because of a back injury, and Davis, her career flagging, surged back into the limelight. Joseph Mankiewicz's elegantly witty screenplay skillfully caught the backstage bitchery of the New York theater scene, and George Sanders, playing a sardonic critic, is seen here introducing his evening date (Marilyn Monroe) at Channing's party, explaining to all that she is a graduate of the Copacabana School of Acting.
All About Eve, 1950.
Director: Joseph L. Mankiewicz.
Starring: Bette Davis, Anne Baxter, George Sanders, Celeste Holm.

All About Eve 1950

Two on a Match

▶ This film transformed cigarette technique, with every small-town Lothario copying Paul Henreid's trick of lighting two and offering one to his partner. On this occasion he preferred the conventional approach. Bette Davis is a repressed, dowdy heiress who is sent on a cruise to avoid a nervous breakdown, where she meets the unhappily married Henreid, with whom she blossoms and enjoys love for the first time. Of course, the romance is doomed but a long, long time later some kind of fulfillment occurs for her, causing the utterance of the great last line, uttered against the plangent surge of Max Steiner's score: "Jerry—don't let's ask for the moon. We have the stars."
Now, Voyager, 1942.
Director: Irving Rapper.
Starring: Bette Davis, Paul Henreid, Claude Rains.

The Big Kiss

▲ At a time when the Hollywood production code stipulated that a screen kiss could last no longer than three seconds Alfred Hitchcock managed to spin out the clinch between Cary Grant and Ingrid Bergman to more than three minutes. He got away with it because he had them speaking lines between mouthfuls, so that the extended moment is really a series of kisses — at one point Grant even takes a phone call. He plays an American agent on the trail of a group of Nazis who have fled the defeated Third Reich for Rio where the hellbrew is bubbling anew. Bergman has been coerced into acting undercover by marrying a leading member of the group. She and Grant fall in love, which throws his professional sense into jeopardy.
Notorious, 1946.
Director: Alfred Hitchcock.
Starring: Cary Grant, Ingrid Bergman, Claude Rains.

"You're not very tall, either"

◀ Bogie and Bacall, here joshing the police department from his office, were besotted by the time they made the Raymond Chandler thriller, and the clever lines (William Faulkner, Jules Furthman, and Leigh Brackett wrote the screenplay) zinged back and forth between them. The plotline was so muddled that even Chandler didn't know who murdered the Sternwood chauffeur, telling Howard Hawks, the director, to figure it out for himself. Bogart, taunted by the statuesque Bacall for his slight build, may not have been the tallest Philip Marlowe, but in his hands the celebrated private eye fulfilled the Chandlerian concept of duty, while keeping a sharp eye on the women along the way, most notably Bacall as the heiress Carmen Sternwood.
The Big Sleep, 1946.
Director: Howard Hawks.
Starring: Humphrey Bogart, Lauren Bacall.

Strangers in the Night

▶ A Noel Coward playlet, Still Life, was the source of this tender British film in which a middle-class suburban housewife, making her weekly pilgrimage to town, meets a doctor at the station when an engine smut lodges in her eye. They talk, meet again, fall in love, try to consummate their affair, know that it is hopeless, and part forever. As the strains of Rachmaninov's Piano Concerto No. 2 swell on the soundtrack, the train draws out, carrying her back to her calm domesticity and placid husband, while her lover sets out on a new life of healing in Africa. Given the restrained acting of Celia Johnson and Trevor Howard it is a noble tearjerker and an early triumph for its young director.
Brief Encounter, 1945.
Director: David Lean.
Starring: Trevor Howard, Celia Johnson, Cyril Raymond, Stanley Holloway.

A Taste for White Water

▲ It is 1914. Humphrey Bogart is a sozzled river rat, Katharine Hepburn a missionary's sister, and this unlikely partnership navigates a beaten-up little steamer down a treacherous African river with the intention of engaging a German warship that is patrolling a lake at the other end. The mismatched pair have many adventures, become lovers, and even reach their objective. Location shooting in Africa was fraught, with almost everyone succumbing to fever except Bogart and Huston who cheerfully boozed instead of drinking the water, which was afterwards found to be contaminated. Bogart won his only Oscar, and Hepburn made sense of her role by playing it like Eleanor Roosevelt.
The African Queen, 1951.
Director: John Huston.
Starring: Humphrey Bogart, Katharine Hepburn, Robert Morley.

Three on a Spree

◄ Truffaut's most popular film is his celebration of youthful joie de vivre in Paris before World War I ended a Bohemian idyll. Oskar Werner, German and Jewish, and Henri Serre, French and his best friend, are artists who fall in love with the Circe-like Jeanne Moreau, who playfully captivates them both, and the trio romps as the world prepares to explode. In the war the men join opposite sides and the ensuing peace grows darker, with quarrels, parting, and tragedy lying ahead. It is far better to remember the early days when life was fun.
Jules and Jim, 1961.
Director: François Truffaut.
Starring: Jeanne Moreau, Oskar Werner, Henri Serre.

Read All About It

▲ Jean-Paul Belmondo, as an amoral small-time hood whose idol is Humphrey Bogart, meets Jean Seberg, a penniless American student peddling newspapers on the Champs-Elysées. They'll become lovers, but she will betray him to the cops because that's the way she is. François Truffaut got the idea from a newspaper clipping. Too busy to turn it into a film himself, he passed it to his Cahiers du Cinéma pal Jean-Luc Godard. The result was the key work of the French New Wave, a ground-breaking liberation from prevailing conventions of filmmaking, with jump cuts, freeze frames, overlapping dialogue, and other items from a cinematic bag of tricks.
Breathless (À Bout de Souffle), 1959.
Director: Jean-Luc Godard.
Starring: Jean-Paul Belmondo, Jean Seberg, Daniel Boulanger.

Beach Parties

◀ The sergeant engages in a torrid affair with the captain's promiscuous wife in the film version of James Jones's sweeping military epic set in Hawaii at the time of Pearl Harbor. Burt Lancaster and Deborah Kerr enacted their famous seduction scene in lapping waves on a sandy shore and, in spite of their discomfort from the sharp granules, created the film's most memorable image. Kerr's part was originally assigned to Joan Crawford, who backed out in the belief it would make her dowdy. Kerr, hitherto renowned for playing cool upper-class types, seized the role of the tramp, forever changing moviegoers' perception of her.
From Here to Eternity, 1953.
Director: Fred Zinnemann.
Starring: Burt Lancaster, Deborah Kerr,
Montgomery Clift, Frank Sinatra.

This is Mr. Norman Maine

◀ A drunken, washed-up movie actor wrecks his actress-wife's acceptance speech on Oscar night by barging on stage to demand recognition from the producers who have cold-shouldered him. James Mason and Judy Garland excelled in the best version of a well-worn Hollywood story, already filmed twice before, with Fredric March and Janet Gaynor in 1937, and Lowell Sherman and Constance Bennett in 1932, when it was called What Price Hollywood? Oddly, that version had the same director as this one. In 1983 a restoration of Cukor's film opened, with excised sequences reinstated, but he had died the night before.
A Star is Born, 1954.
Director: George Cukor.
Starring: Judy Garland, James Mason,
Jack Carson, Charles Bickford, Tom Noonan.

Skirts Ahoy

▲ Marilyn Monroe copes with the long, hot New York summer by keeping her undies in the ice box and standing over a subway grating to catch the breeze from a passing train. "Sort of cools the ankles, doesn't it," observes Tom Ewell, a flirtatious August bachelor whose wife and children are vacationing on a cool lakeshore. The scene had to filmed on a Hollywood soundstage, after a location attempt outside the Trans-Lux theater stalled traffic.
The Seven Year Itch, 1955.
Director: Billy Wilder.
Starring: Marilyn Monroe, Tom Ewell, Evelyn Keyes.

Show a Leg

▶ Here Gable is an average man who doesn't need a college education to know how to dunk a doughnut, while Colbert is a runaway heiress who has never dunked in her life. Breeding aside, she had the advantage in thumbing a ride. Using feminine pragmatism, she hoists her tailored skir above a delicious silk-stockinged knee, stopping a car in its tracks.
It Happened One Night, 1934.
Director: Frank Capra.
Starring: Claudette Colbert, Clark Gable, Roscoe Karns.

Are You Trying to Seduce Me, Mrs Robinson?

◀ Dustin Hoffman was almost thirty when he played Benjamin Braddock, the nervous, bewildered youth beset by advice from his parents' friends after his university graduation. To compound his angst, he discovers that Mrs. Robinson, a close family friend (Anne Bancroft) and the mother of Elaine, the girl he fancies, is anxious to initiate him into sex with an older woman. He finds himself trying simultaneously to satisfy both mother and daughter, and has to make his choice. A funny and immensely popular film, it carried the unspoken message that in time Ben and Elaine would end up exactly like their middle-class suburbanite parents.

The Graduate, 1967.
Director: Mike Nichols.
Starring: Dustin Hoffman, Anne Bancroft, Katharine Ross.

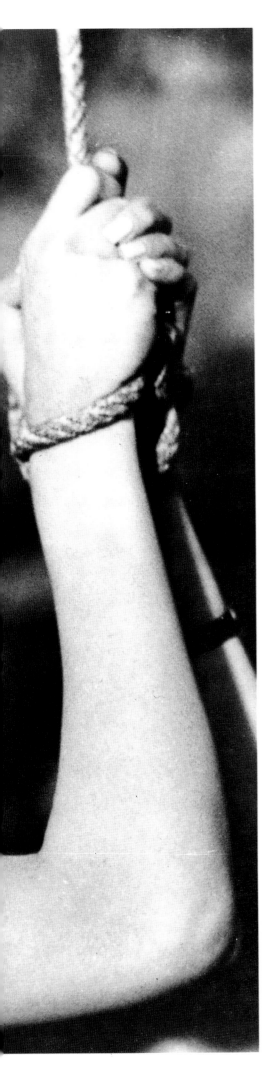

Lash in the Afternoon

◀ The fantasy dream of Severine (Catherine Deneuve), a wealthy, bored Parisian wife, is to be driven to a wood, tied to a tree, with her dress then torn asunder in preparation for a sensuous whipping by the coachman. In her waking moments she relieves her tedium by taking an afternoon job at a luxurious bordello, where as "Belle de Jour" she satisfies the yens of a few expensive clients. Will her insipid husband (Jean Sorel) discover her curious secret? Buñuel's film incisively mocks the bourgeoisie and is an erotic tease, constantly threatening to cross the threshold of pornography yet always staying within urbane tastefulness.
Belle de Jour, 1967.
Director: Luis Buñuel.
Starring: Catherine Deneuve, Jean Sorel, Michel Piccoli, Genevieve Page.

Buttering Up

▲ Brando's career, often controversial, became notorious with this erotic film in which he played an aging American expatriate who, after his wife's suicide, uses a French girl (Maria Schneider) to fulfill his need for sexual contact as solace. The shocking element is the girl's passive acquiescence to rape and sodomy (which is where the butter comes in). The coupling takes place in an empty apartment where they meet by chance while househunting. The passage of time, now that its sensationalism is forgotten, reveals this as a great film, exploring the human psyche with unaccustomed boldness. Brando's performance, occasionally ad-libbed, has an emotional impact that few actors could attain.
Last Tango in Paris, 1972.
Director: Bernardo Bertolucci.
Starring: Marlon Brando, Maria Schneider, Jean-Pierre Léaud.

Figureheads

▼ Lovers Leonardo DiCaprio, from steerage, and Kate Winslet, an upper-deck passenger, ecstatically contemplate the view from the prow, standing in a dangerous position that on most ocean liners would be almost impossible for anyone but an intrepid crew member to reach, but who can speak for the arrangements that existed on the ill-fated Titanic? The filmmakers built their version of the ship in Mexico, and the extended production was one of the most troubled ever. It hardly mattered when it became the first film to gross $1.25 billion.
Titanic, 1997.
Director: James Cameron.
Starring: Leonardo DiCaprio, Kate Winslet, Billy Zane, Frances Fisher, Kathy Bates.

Queen Christina 1933

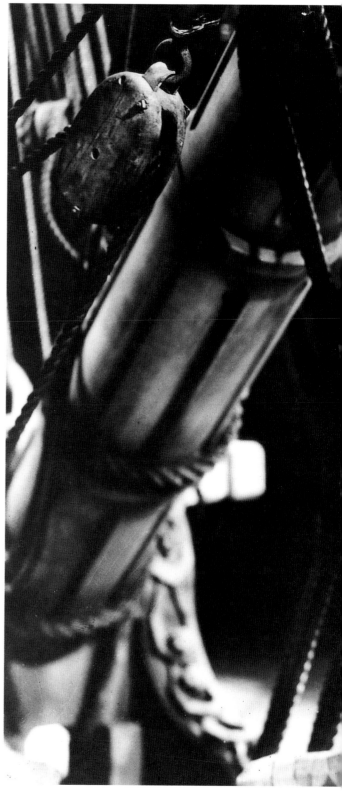

Titanic 1997

Sailing Away

▲ Grief-stricken but proud, the abdicated Swedish queen (Greta Garbo) sails off to Spain, her lover's body aboard the ship. The director Rouben Mamoulian told her to avoid blinking her eyes. "Be nothing but a beautiful mask." The actress complied, and in this classic last moment of the film convinced audiences that she was contemplating a lonely future. The effect was wonderful, except that the breeze stirred her hair, giving the impression that she was sailing into the wind, a difficult feat even given her regal power.
Queen Christina, 1933.
Director: Rouben Mamoulian.
Starring: Greta Garbo, John Gilbert.

Berlin Farewell

▼ "Life is a cabaret, old chum," sings Liza Minnelli, effortlessly gliding toward an Oscar for her first musical role. Bob Fosse's direction of the Kander and Ebb Broadway hit translated the frenzied twilight of Weimar Germany just before the Nazis ascended to power into one of the best of all film musicals. Christopher Isherwood drew on his own experiences for a story collection, Goodbye to Berlin, which was transformed into the stage play I Am a Camera and the musical. Sally Bowles, originally English, is now American, but she is still a naive sophisticate caught up in the turbulence of the era, performing in one of the nightclubs that will soon be obliterated for fermenting decadence as well as free speech.
Cabaret, 1972.
Director: Bob Fosse.
Starring: Liza Minnelli, Michael York, Helmut Griem, Joel Grey.

Fleshy Temptress

◀ In Germany's first talkie, Marlene Dietrich, as Lola-Lola, sings Falling in Love Again in a nightclub cellar into which comes a stuffy high-school teacher (Emil Jannings) intent to put a stop to the outings his students are making, to the detriment of their studies. Instead he is captivated and ensnared, entering a downward path that eventually leads to subjugation and humiliation. Dietrich reluctantly took the role, the director Josef von Sternberg having wanted Brigitte Helm. It made her an international star and was the beginning of a relationship with Sternberg that shaped her early Hollywood career as a sadistic temptress.
The Blue Angel, 1930.
Director: Josef von Sternberg.
Starring: Marlene Dietrich, Emil Jannings, Hans Albers.

Ready for My Close-up

▶ It is the finale. The press corps witness the arrest of the deranged Norma Desmond (Gloria Swanson), who has murdered her reluctant lover, but she imagines that she is back on a movie set about to do a close-up. Amazingly, Swanson was not the first choice to play the forgotten movie diva. Billy Wilder and his screenwriting colleague Charles Brackett originally had Mae West in mind, but she showed them the door when the word "comeback" was mentioned, telling them she had never been away. Swiftly rendering their Hollywood satire darker, they then tried Mary Pickford, but somehow the idea of the World's Sweetheart having a kept man failed to gel. A friend, George Cukor, suggested von Stroheim (left), playing her butler, ex-husband, and former director, the last echoing Swanson's silent film Queen Kelly, which was abandoned when she removed von Stroheim from his directorial chair.
Sunset Boulevard, 1950.
Director: Billy Wilder.
Starring: Gloria Swanson, William Holden, Erich von Stroheim, Nancy Olson.

Gilda 1946

La Dolce Vita 1960

Never a Woman Like Her

◄ "Put the blame on Mame, boys," sings Rita Hayworth, performing a striptease without removing more than a glove in the sexiest number she ever delivered on screen. The story – a trite triangular melodrama set in Buenos Aires with Glenn Ford as the lover who comes between her and her nightclub proprietor husband, George Macready – was forgettable. Hayworth, strutting her stuff in a slinky, strapless, gravity-defying evening gown by Jean Louis, decidedly was not. For the record, the singing voice emanating from those rich full lips was that of Anita Ellis.
Gilda, 1946.
Director: Charles Vidor.
Starring: Rita Hayworth, Glenn Ford, George Macready.

Cool Off in the Fountain

◄ A gossip writer (Marcello Mastroianni) escorts an upholstered Hollywood sex goddess in the making (Anita Ekberg) on a sightseeing tour of Rome. It's a hot night, so she hops blissfully into the cool water of the Trevi Fountain, a move not approved by the municipality who only want tourists to throw in their money. It seems the stunt was Ekberg's own idea, eagerly embraced by Fellini, whose aim in the film was to satirize the cheap banality of social glitz. It was the film that coined the term "paparazzi" for freelance photographers who specialize in candid shots of celebrities.
La Dolce Vita, 1960.
Director: Federico Fellini.
Starring: Marcello Mastroianni, Anita Ekberg, Anouk Aimée.

Water Nymph

◄ Emerging from the warm Jamaica waters is the conch-hunting Honeychile Ryder, offering James Bond an eyeful as she shakes herself dry. The first of the lengthy 007 series to reach the screen, it was filmed on a fraction of subsequent budgets yet manages to be one of the superior examples. The Swiss-born actress Ursula Andress, described by the producer Harry Salzman as "beautiful and cheap," found herself playing the first of the ceaseless stream of exotic women Bond encounters on his many adventures. Sean Connery, a little-known Scottish actor, secured the coveted role, although Bond's originator Ian Fleming wanted an actor with a rougher face. Among others considered was Roger Moore, who eventually inherited the role.
Dr. No, 1962.
Director: Terence Young.
Starring: Sean Connery, Joseph Wiseman, Ursula Andress.

Siren of the Nile

◀ Elizabeth Taylor designed her own eye makeup to play Cleopatra, but her elaborate costumes were mostly the work of Irene Sharaff, who, with co-designers Vittorio Nino Novarese and Renie, won an Academy Award. Darryl F. Zanuck's turgid and exorbitant epic was beset by numerous disasters, including Taylor's near-fatal illness, which required emergency surgery, keeping her out for months. Meanwhile, the huge Roman set at London's Pinewood Studios was abandoned and the production switched to the more favorable and appropriate climate of Cinecittà in Rome.
A consequence of the film was the elevation of Taylor and Richard Burton to the status of screen's number one couple.
Cleopatra, 1963.
Director: Joseph L. Mankiewicz.
Starring: Elizabeth Taylor, Richard Burton, Rex Harrison.

Love Amongst the Ruins

▶ Fassbinder's film is set against West Germany's postwar economic renaissance, the *wirtschaftswunder*, and tells the story of a woman (Hanna Schygulla) who marries in wartime, loses her husband to the Russian front, then searches in vain for him among returning soldiers in 1945. He turns up and takes the blame when Maria kills her casual lover as the men fight. While he is imprisoned, she propels herself as an astute businesswoman, attaining power, position, and wealth for his release, which she celebrates by prancing around the house in black lingerie prior to an explosive finale. Fassbinder's admiration of the glossy, impersonal style of the Danish-born Hollywood director Douglas Sirk supplies an element of kitsch that keeps his best film constantly alive.
The Marriage of Maria Braun, 1978.
Director: Rainer Werner Fassbinder.
Starring: Hanna Schygulla, Klaus Loewitsch, Ivan Desny.

White Passion

◀ When Lana Turner appears in her gleaming two-piece playsuit we know that it is camouflage for the blackest of hearts. She is the archetypal femme fatale, plotting with a lover to murder her kindly, aging husband, the proprietor of a roadside eatery, and hijack his life savings. The sordid, twisting tale of betrayal by James M. Cain was acquired in 1934, but the production code prevented it from being filmed. A French version was made in 1939, but more importantly it became Ossessione, Visconti's first film in 1942, regarded as the start of neorealism in Italian cinema. The screenplay of Hollywood's postwar film satisfied the censors, but Tay Garnett's direction managed to reinstate much of the eroticism that was thought to have been safely purged from it.

The Postman Always Rings Twice, 1946.
Director: Tay Garnett.
Starring: Lana Turner, John Garfield,
Cecil Kellaway, Hume Cronyn.

The Postman Always Rings Twice 1946

White Heat

▲ Femme fatale Sharon Stone, seated on a chair facing officers interrogating her about a murder that is identical to the plotline of her novel, teases the detectives first by smoking in a nonsmoking area — "What are you going to do? Charge me with smoking?" — then crosses her legs to reveal momentarily that she isn't wearing panties. Stone alleged that the lack of panties was not her idea and that she did not know about it until the film was finished. So, how can a star go on set to face the camera in a short skirt not knowing that she is pantyless? The question remains unanswered.

Basic Instinct, 1992.
Director: Paul Van Verhoeven.
Starring: Michael Douglas, Sharon Stone,
Jeanne Triplehorn.

Basic Instinct 1992

End of Rico

▲ While Prohibition was still the law of the land, Edward G. Robinson excelled as the hard-boiled Caesar Enrico Bandello. He plays a killer who pushes his way to control a city's underworld in a career trajectory akin to that of Al Capone, still unprosecuted the year the film was released. Little Caesar's luck eventually runs out. Isolated, his wealth and power lost, he falls into a police trap and is gunned down. His nemesis, Lieutenant Flaherty (Thomas Jackson) is able to hear his famous last words: "Mother of mercy... is this the end of Rico?"
Little Caesar, 1930.
Director: Mervyn LeRoy.
Starring: Edward G. Robinson,
Douglas Fairbanks, Jr., Glenda Farrell.

Gun Crazy

▶ Paul Muni played Tony Camonte, another character modeled on Capone, in a film so shockingly violent that a secondary title, The Shame of a Nation, was added for its initial release, as well as a prologue and epilogue pushing a Crime Doesn't Pay line. Over the head of the director, the producer, Howard Hughes, ordered that a scene showing Camonte being tried and hanged be appended. Confusingly, most prints show him gunned down in a gutter. The film was released just as the Eighteenth Amendment was being repealed.
Scarface, 1932.
Director: Howard Hawks.
Starring: Paul Muni, Ann Dvorak, Karen Morley.

Nose Job

▲ Roman Polanski appeared as a minor hood who slices the nose of a private investigator (Jack Nicholson) for sticking it too closely into a Los Angeles water-rights case that is steeped in corruption. A complicated narrative, involving rape, incest, and murder, is subtly incorporated here within the ambience of the thirties, showing what a dismal loss Polanski's self-imposed banishment, following a disgraceful morals charge, has been to Hollywood. Nothing he has made since comes near it in quality.
Chinatown, 1974.
Director: Roman Polanski.
Starring: Jack Nicholson, Faye Dunaway, John Huston.

Making a Hit

▶ In one of the most astonishing comebacks ever, John Travolta became one of Hollywood's highest-paid stars. In this key moment, from the most singular thriller of the nineties, he and Samuel L. Jackson engage in their calling as professional assassins. Tarantino's screenplay bristles with irrelevant discussions on topics such as the Parisian name for a McDonald's quarter-pounder, while the intricate structure, filled with flashbacks from different perspectives, recalls Rashomon. The director famously worked as a clerk in a video store, absorbing movies by the barrel-load, so that scarcely a line lacks an allusion or a prototype.
Pulp Fiction, 1994.
Director: Quentin Tarantino.
Starring: John Travolta, Uma Thurman, Samuel L. Jackson, Harvey Keitel.

Mark of Cain

◀ Fritz Lang's first talking picture made a star of Peter Lorre, hitherto a little-known Hungarian actor the director had spotted in a play in Berlin. Cast as a serial child-murderer who is brought to justice by the underworld itself, his performance is so textured that he makes the tortured soul of the psychopath comprehensible, almost worthy of sympathy. He is tracked down because the chalkmark "M," the sign of a murderer, has been pressed onto his back by a beggar. Lorre's brilliance was to hobble his career. Henceforth he was typecast in deviant roles. Both he and Fritz Lang fled Germany as the Nazis rose to power. Lang had rebuffed an offer to stay to make propaganda films for them. After he left, parts of M were edited out of context to portray Lorre as a degenerate Jew.
M, 1931.
Director: Fritz Lang.
Starring: Peter Lorre, Otto Wermicke.

Goodnight, Vienna

▲ Orson Welles made only fleeting appearances in the Graham Greene postwar thriller set in four-power Vienna, but he stamped his imprint all over it as the villainous Harry Lime. His disappearance sets his shallow American friend, pulp-fiction writer Holly Martins, on a dangerous pursuit, out of his depth, as he tries to solve the mystery. A Viennese zither player called Anton Karas, discovered in a café, was commissioned to compose and pluck the background score on his obscure stringed instrument. With its unusual twanging, the theme reached a prime place in the music charts, abetting the film's success.
The Third Man, 1949.
Director: Carol Reed.
Starring: Joseph Cotten, Trevor Howard, Orson Welles, Alida Valli.

M 1931

The Third Man 1949

Looking for the Bird

▶ The cast unwraps a package containing the black bird, allegedly stuffed with precious jewels. Or does it? George Raft turned down the part of Dashiell Hammett's private eye, Sam Spade, because he was unhappy at the thought of working with an untried director. John Huston had written the screenplay for an earlier Humphrey Bogart picture, High Sierra, which Raft had also declined, but it was this film that elevated the stocky actor into mega-stardom. Peter Lorre and Sydney Greenstreet, oozing epicene bonhomie, were a fine team of villains, although the latter was making his debut at sixty-one. Mary Astor was never better as the femme fatale. Remakes rarely transcend the original. The thriller had been filmed twice before, in 1931 and 1936, but this version rendered both instantly forgettable.
The Maltese Falcon, 1941.
Director: John Huston.
Starring: Humphrey Bogart, Mary Astor, Peter Lorre, Sydney Greenstreet.

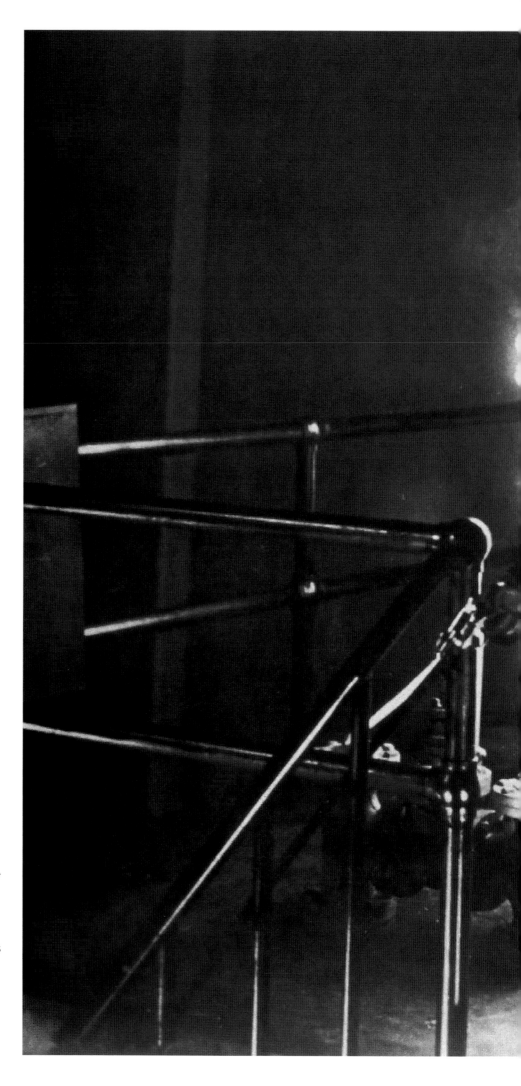

Going Out with a Bang

 "Made it, ma, top of the world," cries Cody Jarrett, the mother-fixated, psychopathic hoodlum played by James Cagney making his exit to hell in a ball of fire as a tank in an oil refinery in Torrance, California, explodes. As a screen gangster Cagney was peerless, and in this memorable thriller he played a character based on the real-life Arthur "Doc" Barker. His other memorable moments include the emptying of a gun into the rear of a car when the victim in the trunk complains of inadequate ventilation and tearing apart a crowded prison mess hall in a berserk fit after news reaches him of his mother's death.
White Heat, 1949.
Director: Raoul Walsh.
Starring: James Cagney, Virginia Mayo, Edmond O'Brien, Margaret Wycherly.

Make My Day

◀ The Bill of Rights can go hang when Harry Callahan is around. Clint Eastwood's San Francisco cop acts like a frontier vigilante, eliminating bad elements with his ever-ready Magnum 45 and saving the public the expense of trial time. Somehow Dirty Harry fitted the ugly mood of the time when Richard Nixon sat in the White House and right-wing groups argued that the liberals had been too permissive, leaving society exposed. The character reflected that mood, and in his quest to destroy an ugly serial killer called Scorpio Eastwood is so good an actor he convinces the audience that he is right and the law's demand for due process is wrong. The theater marquee billing Eastwood's first film as director is there for the true fans.

Dirty Harry, 1971.
Director: Don Siegel.
Starring: Clint Eastwood, Harry Guardino, Reni Santoni.

Chock Full of Shots

▼ The crime spree of the bank-robbing couple Clyde Barrow and Bonnie Parker, whose exploits across rural America fed newspaper headlines during the Depression, ended in a bloody police ambush near Gibsland, Louisiana. It was recreated in painful slow motion as the climax of Arthur Penn's graphic film, with Warren Beatty tumbling from the automobile. Faye Dunaway's leg was tied to the gearshift so that her fall would take place after his. David Newman and Robert Benton's screenplay was largely fictitious. Here, following an ambush and a violent police chase, Beatty tumbles from the driver's seat, wounded in the arm. Gang members Gene Hackman and Estelle Parsons are in back of the car.
Bonnie and Clyde, 1967.
Director: Arthur Penn.
Starring: Warren Beatty, Faye Dunaway, Michael J. Pollard, Gene Hackman.

Won by a Head

▶ Mario Puzo's epic study of the Mafia from the inside produced three superlative movies, this one in 1972, with sequels following in 1974 and 1990. The first was dominated by Marlon Brando as Don Vito Corleone, with his wheezy instruction to cohorts to do his bidding and "make him an offer he can't refuse." Johnny Fontane, a singer and friend of the family, needs a break in Hollywood, but Jack Woltz (John Marley), a movie boss, is blocking him. Woltz awakes in the middle of the night to find himself covered in blood, then discovers that he is sharing his bed with the head of his cherished racehorse. He is persuaded and Fontane gets his break.
The Godfather, 1972.
Director: Francis Ford Coppola.
Starring: Marlon Brando, Al Pacino, James Caan, Richard Conte, Diane Keaton.

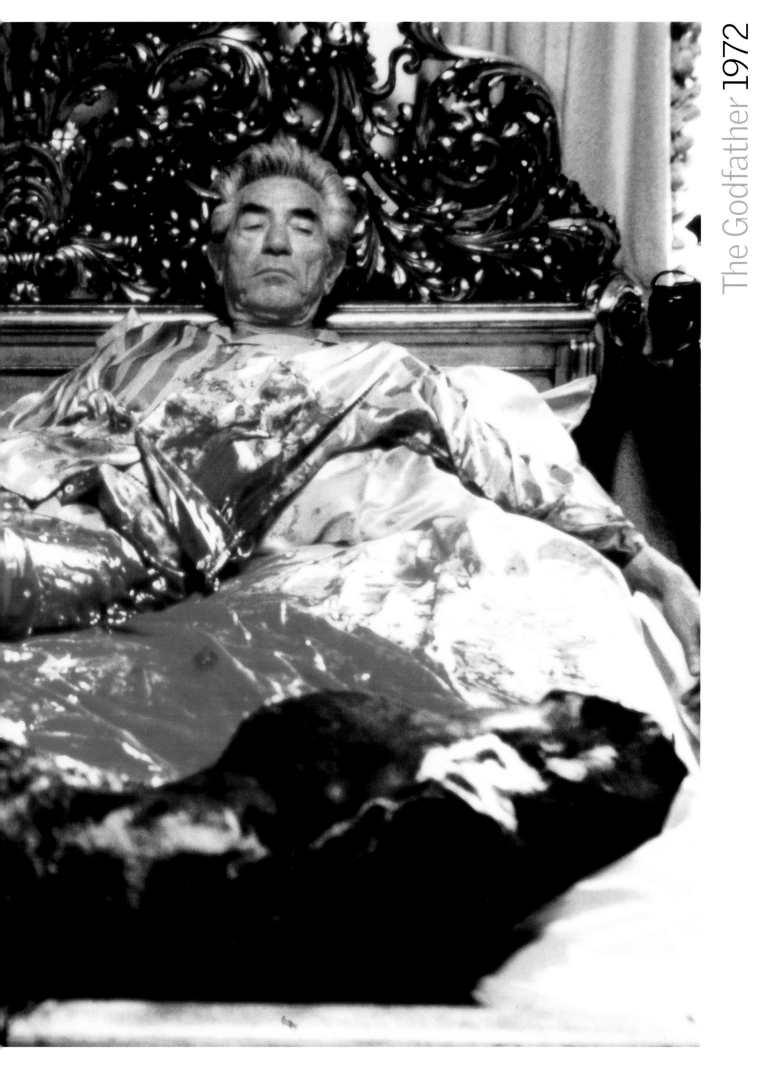

Girl Power

◀ Trapped in dull partnerships with indifferent
men, best friends Susan Sarandon and Geena Davis
decide to take to the road from Arkansas in a 1956
Thunderbird for no other reason than to get out of
their rut for two or three days. The female-buddy
breakout quickly goes sour when an intending
rapist in a parking lot is killed, and the women
have to take flight for real. Soon they are on all
the wanted lists and the cops are closing in
as they drive the dusty roads of the Southwest.
It would be a cliché if they weren't women.
Back in Arkansas one of the lawmen
(Harvey Keitel) monitors their progress and
forms a kind of empathy with their discovery of
freedom, which he knows is only an illusion.
Thelma and Louise, 1991.
Director: Ridley Scott.
Starring: Geena Davis, Susan Sarandon,
Harvey Keitel, Michael Madsen.

Stopped in his Tracks

▲ The climax of this movie is one of the most exciting chases ever filmed. Gene Hackman as Popeye Doyle, a manic NYPD narcotics detective, pursues a hit man (Marcello Bozuffi) who has fled the crime scene on an elevated train. Doyle commandeers a car and drives at breakneck speed on the crowded streets below. The assassin, having killed a transit cop, leaps from the now-crashed train and falls to Doyle's gun. Hackman's character was based on a massively successful drug-busting New York cop, Eddie Egan, who was technical adviser. The NYPD prematurely retired him because of "image problems," leading to his new career in Hollywood.
The French Connection, 1971.
Director: William Friedkin.
Starring: Gene Hackman, Fernando Rey, Roy Scheider.

No Wonder I Feel Dizzy

▶ Hitchcock was the first to use the reverse zoom, now a trick in every TV ad-director's manual, with the camera dollying out and zooming in simultaneously, an effect that simulated James Stewart's acrophobia (fear of heights) as he made his way down a mission tower staircase.
In Hitchcock's most complex and absorbing thriller he plays a retired police detective whose private client's wife has apparently fallen to her death, causing him to become obsessively anxious to recreate her image from another woman.
The key edifice, the tower of San Juan Bautista south of San Francisco, was a Hitchcock fiction. The real one collapsed in the 1906 earthquake.
Vertigo, 1958.
Director: Alfred Hitchcock.
Starring: James Stewart, Kim Novak, Barbara Bel Geddes.

Vertigo 1958

Rendezvous for Kaplan

◀ Grant, as Roger O. Thornhill, a New York adman, has been mistaken by spies for a double agent called Kaplan, sending him on a frantic journey across America, pursued by enemy assassins, police, and secret services, each with a different motive. The dazzling climax will take place on the carved presidential faces of Mount Rushmore. Alfred Hitchcock loved setting challenges for himself. Another director would have staged the attempt on Cary Grant's life at night in a dark alleyway with wet cobblestones glistening in subdued lamplight. Hitch reversed all that in a brilliant, unforgettable, yet utterly crazy sequence. There have been easier ways to kill someone than by luring him to an open prairie and strafing him from a crop-dusting airplane. The cornfield, meant to be somewhere in the Midwest, was actually near Bakersfield, California.
North by Northwest, 1959.
Director: Alfred Hitchcock.
Starring: Cary Grant, Eva Marie Saint, James Mason.

North by Northwest 1959

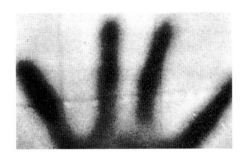

Stay Out of the Shower

◀ Saul Bass storyboarded the most famous shower scene in movies, but Alfred Hitchcock directed it. That is the truth according to Janet Leigh, who was there most of the time, except when her body double, Marli Renfro, provided her nude torso for the more than 70 setups required to show the frenzied knife murder. Whatever audiences thought they saw, the knife never penetrated flesh. Hitchcock always regarded his masterly horror film as a black comedy, and killing off the leading lady so early on was part of the joke.
Psycho, 1960.
Director: Alfred Hitchcock.
Starring: Anthony Perkins, Janet Leigh, Vera Miles, John Gavin.

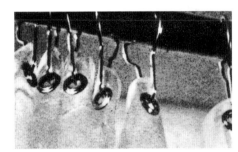

Psycho 1960

Night Caller

◀ Father Merrin (Max von Sydow), a Jesuit priest, comes to a house in Georgetown to confront Satan, who is in possession of a twelve-year-old girl. The film adaptation of William Peter Blatty's dark novel, based on an exorcism case in 1949 when he was a student at Georgetown University, has the reputation of being the most frightening ever made. The special effects that cause the child (Linda Blair) to levitate, convulse, inflate, spew green slime, and, most terrifying of all, turn her head full circle were trailblazers for many imitators. So many accidents and even deaths impeded the shooting that the production itself was deemed possessed. If so, the box office was spared. On release it became the fifth-biggest grosser of all time.
The Exorcist, 1973.
Director: William Friedkin.
Starring: Ellen Burstyn, Max von Sydow, Jason Miller, Lee J. Cobb.

The Axeman Cometh

▲ In Kubrick's lengthy, thinly populated occult thriller from a Stephen King best seller, Jack Nicholson plays a writer who has taken a winter job as a caretaker in a mountain resort hotel in Colorado during the snowbound months when it's closed. Grisly past events have produced ghosts that unhinge Nicholson, who spends a huge amount of screen time armed with an axe stalking his wife (Shelley Duvall) and five-year-old son through endless, empty corridors. In this memorable moment, he breaks down the door of a room in which they are cowering, with the cry "He-e-e-e-re's Johnny!"
The Shining, 1980.
Director: Stanley Kubrick.
Starring: Jack Nicholson, Shelley Duvall, Danny Lloyd, Scatman Crothers.

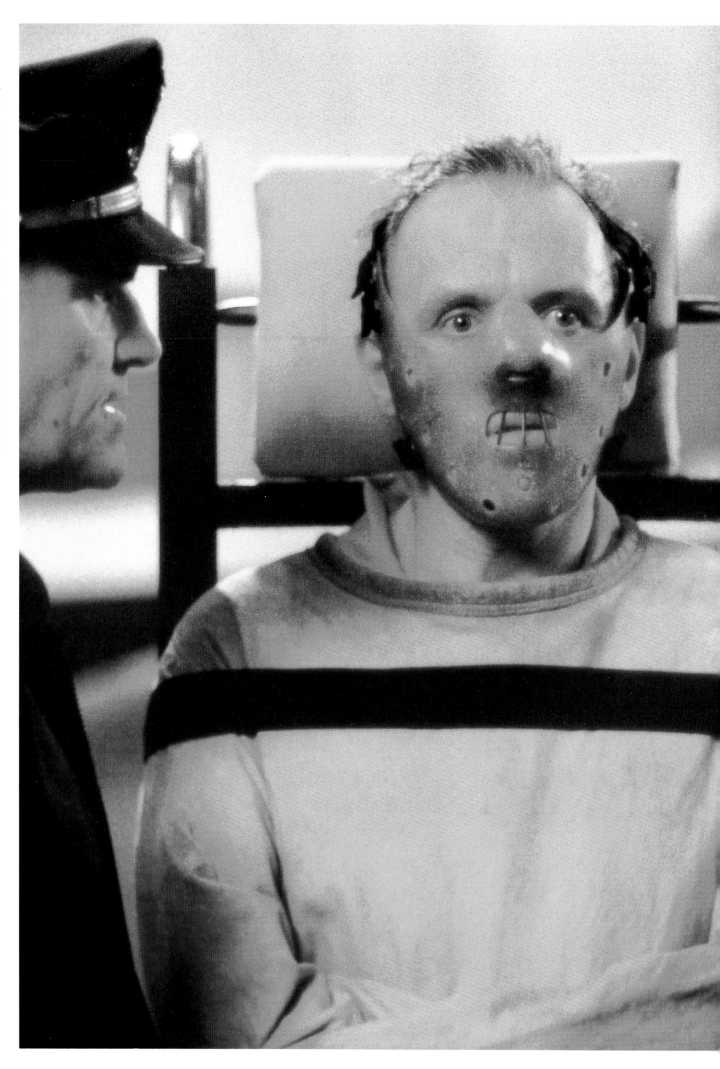

Hannibal the Cannibal

◄ Anthony Hopkins is the superintelligent Dr. Hannibal Lecter, incarcerated under high security after his conviction as a serial killer who eats his victims. Agent Starling of the FBI (Jodie Foster) persuades him to help catch another murderer, called Buffalo Bill, by empathizing with him. In spite of the elaborate restraint methods employed to keep Lecter secure, he terrifies those whose duty it is to guard him — not without reason, since mentally he is so many steps ahead that he can still outwit them all with the power of his evil.
The Silence of the Lambs 1991.
Director: Jonathan Demme.
Starring: Anthony Hopkins, Jodie Foster, Scott Glen.

"Are You Talkin' to Me?"

▲ Driving a cab around Manhattan at night could destroy a man's soul, especially if he was already halfway there, like Vietnam Marine veteran Travis Bickle (Robert De Niro). The urban squalor of the Time Square district in the 1970s, with its drug-pushers, hard-core movie houses, and underage hookers, affects him to the point of insanity, and his murderous explosion is an expression of anger and disgust. De Niro's performance as an isolated man is mesmerizing. Jodie Foster is particularly effective as a child prostitute in hot pants whom he tries to rescue. At one point Martin Scorsese himself is his passenger, playing a man tracking his wife to another man's apartment.
Taxi Driver, 1976.
Director: Martin Scorsese.
Starring: Robert De Niro, Cybill Shepherd, Jodie Foster, Harvey Keitel.

Time's Up

 Harold Lloyd didn't have a particular head for heights but appreciated the comic possibilities of a man dangling from a high building. He had used thrills in a few shorts, but Safety Last was his first feature to include a nail-biting sequence. The idea occurred when he saw a "human fly" ascend a Los Angeles building. He hired him to appear in the far long shots, but he did all the rest himself. A false front explains the curious perspective of the street behind him, but even so his safety platform was nearly useless three stories below. Lloyd's courage was remarkable. He also had a severely mutilated hand from a bomb stunt that went wrong in another film and wore a prosthetic glove.

Safety Last, 1923.
Directors: Fred Newmeyer, Sam Taylor.
Starring: Harold Lloyd, Mildred Davis,
Bill Strothers.

Sole Comfort

◄ Marooned by blizzards in an icy cabin, Charlie Chaplin serves up a Thanksgiving dinner for himself and his fellow prospector Mack Swain – his cooked shoe. The laces become spaghetti, the sole a delicate fish to be boned carefully. Swain reverses the plates so that he has the more succulent upper. The boots were actually made of licorice. Chaplin, ever the perfectionist, had 20 pairs made, to Swain's horror when the laxative side effects became apparent. It is not the only starvation joke. Later Swain, driven temporarily insane by hunger, visualizes Chaplin as a giant chicken and chases him around the cabin with a gun. It was Chaplin's first starring feature under the banner of United Artists banner, the company he had co-founded with Pickford, Fairbanks, and Griffith.
The Gold Rush, 1925.
Director: Charles Chaplin.
Starring: Charles Chaplin, Georgia Hale, Mack Swain.

Battle Lines

◀ For his silent masterpiece Buster Keaton used an actual incident from the Civil War in which a train was hijacked from Atlanta by Union soldiers on the loose and driven to Chattanooga, creating havoc en route. Keaton played a Southerner, rejected from military service because his job as a railroad engineer was too valuable. His locomotive, The General, and the train, with his fiancée on board, are seized by Union spies, but he pursues them in another locomotive, overcoming innumerable obstacles such as crossties strewn across the track. Riding on the cowcatcher, he uses the tie he clutches to flip away one in front of the train, just in the nick of time, a stunt that invariably provokes applause at screenings.
The General, 1926.
Director: Buster Keaton.
Starring: Buster Keaton, Marion Mack, Jim Farley.

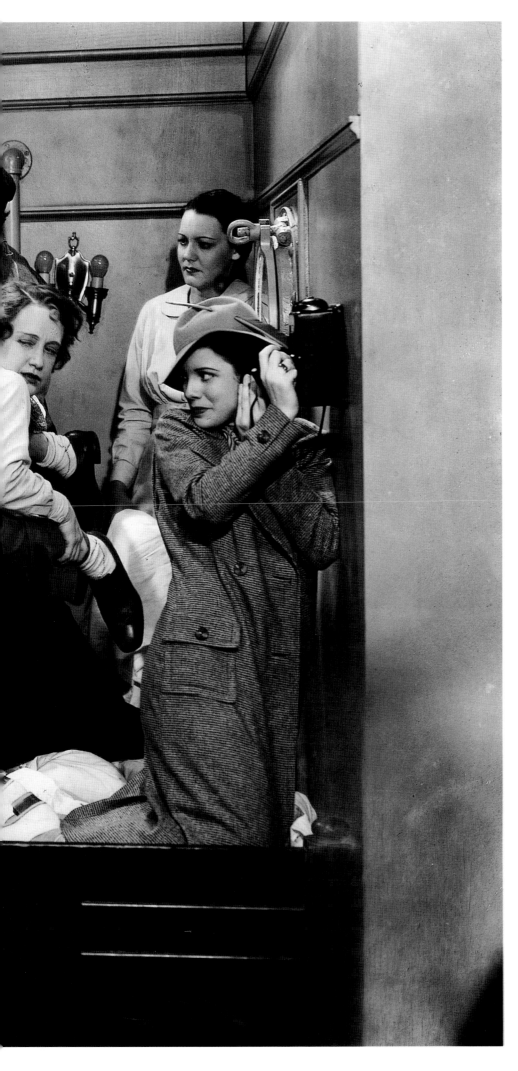

Room for No More

◄ Just how many people it is possible to cram into a small stateroom on an ocean liner was famously tested when Groucho's cabin, already containing Chico, Harpo, and Zeppo, was invaded by workmen, waiters, maids, cleaners, and a young woman looking for her Aunt Minny. The coup de grace is applied by the buxom Margaret Dumont as a society grande dame who is being duped by Groucho. As she opens the door, a massive explosion of humanity tumbles out on top of her. When they tried it on stage it didn't work. On film it is one of the funniest scenes ever.
A Night at the Opera, 1935.
Director: Sam Wood.
Starring: The Marx Brothers, Margaret Dumont, Kitty Carlisle, Allan Jones.

Cog in the Wheel

▶ Armed with two wrenches, Charlie Chaplin plays a nut-tightener in his satirical comedy on assembly tyranny and its effect on the human spirit. Sound films had by then been around for nearly a decade, but he largely ignores dialogue apart from a nonsense song, preferring to mime his peerless routines to a silent tempo. This was the last time Chaplin's Little Tramp character appeared, playing a victim to the greed of an industrial regime, herded into monotonous assembly-line work, even forced to use a fallible eating machine to speed up his lunch break. The film's anti-capitalist tone provided ammunition for those who would later have Chaplin barred from the U.S. as a Communist, yet this film was deeply unpopular with the U.S.S.R. establishment. The Soviets, with unceasing five-year plans affixed to a multitude of industries, were in no mood to attack mass production.

Modern Times, 1936.
Director: Charles Chaplin.
Starring: Charles Chaplin, Paulette Goddard.

The Way to a Dukedom

▶ The D'Ascoyne family are at prayer, and seven of them, including the doddering figure in the pulpit and the reclining knight on the tomb, are played by Alec Guinness in a clever composite shot that required considerable skill to film. The witty, ironic plot of this sublime black comedy, an Ealing comedy that stands apart from all the others, concerns a disgruntled fringe member (Dennis Price) of a noble family who resolves to murder his way to the dukedom, even though eight others (all Guinness) stand in the way. Worse, having accomplished his goal, he finds himself torn between two captivating women and can only quote John Gay's lines from The Beggar's Opera, "How happy could I be with either, Were t'other dear charmer away."
Kind Hearts and Coronets, 1949.
Director: Robert Hamer.
Starring: Alec Guinness, Dennis Price,
Valerie Hobson, Joan Greenwood.

Kind Hearts and Coronets 1949

These Aren't My Clothes

▲ Cary Grant's explanation to May Robson about why he should be wearing a fluffy negligee has acquired over the years more piquancy than was originally intended in Dudley Nichols's classic screwball screenplay. He declares, "I just went gay all of a sudden!" His plight was actually the consequence of a silly misadventure with Robson's niece, played by Katharine Hepburn. It was the only time Hepburn attempted slapstick comedy, playing a headstrong heiress who moves into the life of a staid paleontologist and proceeds to tear it apart with the ruthless, steely determination of a woman who has suddenly found she is in love. Moviegoers are eternally grateful.
Bringing Up Baby, 1938.
Director: Howard Hawks.
Starring: Katharine Hepburn, Cary Grant, Charlie Ruggles, May Robson.

I'm a Girl

▶ The greatest drag act in movie history was that of Tony Curtis and Jack Lemon in Billy Wilder and I. A. L. Diamond's peerless comedy. As Chicago musicians who inadvertently witness the St. Valentine's Day massacre, they are forced to flee by joining a touring all-girl band and end up in Florida. Disguised as women, they not only appear convincing to Marilyn Monroe, the band's singer, but Lemmon is actively wooed by a millionaire, Joe E. Brown, leading to the tremendous parting line, "Well, nobody's perfect." Diamond thought of it the night before, intending to change it to something better on the set. In the rush it stayed.
Some Like It Hot, 1959.
Director: Billy Wilder.
Starring: Marilyn Monroe, Tony Curtis, Jack Lemmon, George Raft, Joe E. Brown.

Archie in Trouble

▶ John Cleese plays a stuffy English barrister called Archie Leach, a derivative name if ever there was, who falls for the seductive wiles of an American conwoman (Jamie Lee Curtis) and is caught nude (she has kept her clothes on) by a middle-class family calling to view the borrowed premises where the assignation is taking place. In general, the excellent farce, co-written with Cleese and directed by a great veteran of Ealing comedy, evenhandedly sends up the gross side of both the British and American character. Kevin Kline as Curtis's dim-witted accomplice is particularly effective, misinterpreting everything he sees.
A Fish Called Wanda, 1988.
Director: Charles Crichton.
Starring: John Cleese, Jamie Lee Curtis, Kevin Kline, Michael Palin.

The Entertainer 1960

Dead Behind the Eyes

▲ Laurence Olivier repeated his stage triumph as the washed-up British vaudevillian Archie Rice in the film version of John Osborne's play. Rice's third-rate act in a shabby theater in a faded seaside resort attracts few patrons, and his private life is ebbing into decline. It is set in 1956 during the Suez crisis, and the playwright uses Archie as a metaphor for England in decline, clinging hopelessly to past glories. Beneath Archie's cheap greasepaint there is a savage, bitter, and electrifying anger. Olivier used to say that Rice was more him than Hamlet.
The Entertainer, 1960.
Director: Tony Richardson.
Starring: Laurence Olivier, Brenda de Banzie, Joan Plowright, Roger Livesey.

A Robot Walks

▼ Fritz Lang's prophetic epic visualizes a twenty-first century in which the rich cavort on the surface in golden sunlight while workers far below toil ceaselessly in vast subterranean plants.

It is the German silent cinema's visual masterpiece. A crazed scientist (Rudolf Klein-Rogge) creates a feminine robot to lead the masses in revolt, giving it the face of a saintly woman (Brigitte Helm). H. G. Wells hated the film because it foresaw a future in which machines would master people, but Hitler was so impressed he urged Lang to remain in Germany to make Nazi propaganda films. The director declined.
Metropolis, 1926.
Director: Fritz Lang.
Starring: Alfred Abel, Gustav Fröhlich, Rudolf Klein-Rogge, Brigitte Helm.

A Somnabulist Walks

◀ The jagged, angular, painted decor of this famous early exercise in German expressionism was meant to depict the distorted, tortured vision of a madman. Robert Wiene's film, its scenery the work of three eminent painters — Herman Warm, Walter Röhrig, and Walter Reiman — had a profound influence on graphic design during the twenties. The story, of a sinister traveling hypnotist who controls a sleepwalker, commanding him to prowl at night to perform evil deeds, is grotesque. The Nazis denounced the film as "degenerate," ensuring that its reputation would endure.
The Cabinet of Dr. Caligari, 1919.
Director: Robert Wiene.
Starring: Werner Krauss, Conrad Veidt, Lil Dagover.

Come Play With Me

◄ The scene in which Boris Karloff's monster plays
by a lakeside with a little girl, throwing flower
petals into the water, has a horrific climax in which
he drowns her because there are no petals left.
It was deemed too awful for U.S. audiences and
was cut by the studio against Karloff's wishes,
but was shown in his native England. The monster
makeup was torture, taking seven hours a day to
apply and remove. Karloff wore 30-pound weights
in his massive boots, steel rods on his legs, and
a huge extension to his head. It was worth it
to create one of cinema's most enduring icons,
reprised in later films and endlessly parodied.
Frankenstein, 1931.
Director: James Whale.
Starring: Boris Karloff, Colin Clive, Mae Clarke.

Top of the World

◀ The Empire State Building was very new and regarded as the eighth wonder of the world when Kong made his fatal ascent after a destructive rampage through New York. Transplanted monsters running amok in major cities are a movie staple, and Kong was not the first. The Lost World in 1925 had already been there. But it was Kong who defined the genre in a superbly crafted film that belied the difficulties Schoedsack and Cooper endured in the making. Fay Wray's performance as Ann, the human loved by the ape, was a key to the film's success. As the explorer-showman Carl Denham (Robert Armstrong) says over Kong's fallen body: "It wasn't the airplanes. It was beauty killed the beast."
King Kong, 1933.
Directors: Merian C. Cooper, Ernest B. Schoedsack.
Starring: Fay Wray, Robert Armstrong, Bruce Cabot.

Watch the Skies

▲ The mothership hovers over the Devil's Tower, Wyoming, landing site at the climax of Spielberg's science-fiction epic, with the world's scientists, newsmen, and broadcast networks gathered to meet the first definite visitors from outer space. In a curious case of anal retentiveness, Spielberg continued to tamper with the film after its release and persuaded Columbia to invest a further $8 million on his Special Edition, released three years later, essentially a re-edit incorporating outtakes, discarding material that fell flat, and including new, specially shot scenes, among them the interior of the alien ship, which looked like the over-illuminated lobby of a designer hotel.
Close Encounters of the Third Kind, 1977 (and 1980).
Director: Steven Spielberg.
Starring: Richard Dreyfuss, François Truffaut, Teri Garr, Melinda Dillon.

To Boldly Go

▶ Stanley Kubrick's epic vision of turn-of-the-century space travel appeared the year before Neil Armstrong became the first man to set foot on the Moon, yet somehow it defined cosmology for the general public more effectively than the Apollo missions. It also began the tedious method of referring to the beginning of the twenty-first century as "two thousand" rather than "twenty-hundred." His sparse human cast, including Keir Dullea (right), was eclipsed by the powerful beauty of his gently gliding spacecraft and the awful, empty distance between Earth and Jupiter. His film begins and ends with an enigma that threatens but never fulfills an answer to the eternal question of human existence: Why?
2001: A Space Odyssey, 1968.
Director: Stanley Kubrick.
Starring: Keir Dullea, Gary Lockwood, William Sylvester, Leonard Rossiter.

Eye Trouble

▼ One of the most famous shock images in movies is from a silent surrealist short that grabbed attention (or nausea) from the start when a girl's eye was apparently sliced by a razor. Mercifully it belonged to a dead sheep, although fainting audience members at first showings didn't know that. Ants pouring from a hole in a man's hand, which becomes dismembered and causes a commotion in the street, and a decomposing horse atop a grand piano are among the other images that engage the audience. What it does it all mean? Simply, two talented avant-gardist young men (Dali and Buñuel) having fun.
Un Chien Andalou, 1928.
Directors: Salvador Dali, Luis Buñuel.
Starring: Salvador Dali, Luis Buñuel.

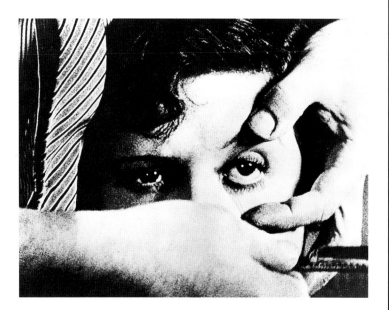

Bring on the Ultra-V

▶ The horrific leering image of Malcolm McDowell lounging in a milk bar in his "droog" outfit became the overall motif as well as the opening shot of Kubrick's astonishing version of the novel by Anthony Burgess. Some perceived it as an incitement to violence, with a delinquent gang engaging in an almost ritualistic routine of beating and raping the innocents who cross their path. In fact, it demonstrates that, when it comes to ruthlessness, the government outstrips mere individuals. Kubrick, a resident of England for nearly 40 years, was so anxious not to offend British sensibilities that he exercised draconian self-censorship and refused to allow any screenings there after the initial release, a decision posthumously rescinded.
A Clockwork Orange, 1971.
Director: Stanley Kubrick.
Starring: Malcolm McDowell, Patrick Magee, Michael Bates.

Un Chien Andalou 1928

A Galaxy Far Away

▲ Alec Guinness as Ben (Obi-Wan) Kenobi fights his duel by light saber with Darth Vader, a former knight of the Jedi who has turned to the dark side and is about to sacrifice his life so that the Force, the mysterious power that imparts huge strength and perception to those who are endowed with it, can transfer to the young hero Luke Skywalker, enabling him to destroy the Death Star. The storyline borrows heavily from many movie-buff sources, from Ford's The Searchers to Kurosawa's The Hidden Fortress, with a vigorous dash of Flash Gordon serials, but it has a special quality of its own that made it an instant mega-success, with two sequels and, to date, one prequel.
Star Wars, 1977.
Director: George Lucas.
Starring: Mark Hamill, Harrison Ford,
Alec Guinness, Carrie Fisher

Keeping the Ball Rolling

▶ The nod toward Saturday matinee adventure yarns was obvious even from the main title with its comic-book lettering. In the role of Indiana Jones, Harrison Ford instantly made archaeology the most thrilling profession in the world. The mood is established in this opening sequence, detached Bond-style from the main plot, in which Indy enters a tomb filled with hidden traps, including this massive stone ball that bears down on him. The rest of the story, set in the 1930s, is concerned with thwarting a Nazi attempt to steal the Ark of the Covenant and its sacred contents, the tablets bearing the Ten Commandments. Sequels and a television spinoff were inevitable following the film's huge box-office triumph.
Raiders of the Lost Ark, 1981.
Director: Steven Spielberg.
Starring: Harrison Ford, Karen Allen,
Paul Freeman, Ronald Lacey.

Star Wars 1977

134

Looking for a Phone

◀ At Halloween a small boy has the best friend he could ever hope for, a wise, sweet creature from a distant planet who has been stranded on Earth but sadly cannot survive for long in its atmosphere. Hidden in the depths of the nearby forest is equipment that can enable the alien to "phone home." With a combination of human pedal power and extraterrestrial telekinesis the boy and his passenger soar over the trees to their goal. The entrancing long-lens image of the pair silhouetted against a giant moon is repeated later when a whole squadron of children on bikes sailed skyward as they try to outwit the adult forces of reason that want to capture and kill E. T. to examine him as a biological specimen. Spielberg later adapted this image as the logo for his production company Amblin Entertainment.

E. T. The Extra-Terrestrial, 1982.
Director: Steven Spielberg.
Starring: Dee Wallace, Henry Thomas, Peter Coyote.

One in the Eye

▲ Georges Méliès was one of the first to appreciate that movies were magical, appropriately for the owner of the Robert Houdin theater, where the great nineteenth-century illusionist had presented his celebrated optical tricks. Méliès began projecting films in 1896 and was soon making his own. Only a handful of the hundreds he supervised survive, and his career dwindled away as his style became dated and interest faded. Today the ingenuity of his special effects, mostly created within the camera by stop motion, seems extraordinarily appealing, and often his rudimentary science fiction has a touch of Gallic frivolity, such as this lunar expedition, which discovers that the Moon is inhabited by lightly-clad chorus girls.

A Trip to the Moon, 1902.
Director: Georges Méliès.

A Man Could Fall

▼ Bruce Willis, dangling from a fire hose, smashes through a plate glass window 50 stories above the street into a high-rise office building that has been hijacked by terrorists. Willis, as a New York cop on furlough in Los Angeles, stumbles on the plot and becomes a one-man counterstrike force against a well-armed, well-organized enemy. So successful was his new persona that sequels inevitably followed. Two years later Willis played a New York cop temporarily in Washington, D.C., where he accidentally stumbles on a terrorist plot that he must deal with as a virtual one-man band. At one point he asks, "How can the same thing happen to the same guy twice?" Because the box office says so, dummy.
Die Hard, 1988.
Director: John McTiernan.
Starring: Bruce Willis, Bonnie Bedelia, Alan Rickman.

A Man Can Fly?

◀ Christopher Reeve soars through the air in superhero mode as the popular comic-book champion of the oppressed. Outstanding in four Superman films, Reeve later had a horse-riding accident that left him permanently paralyzed from the neck down. His courage and dogged fight to survive and have a life, even with occasional acting appearances, has given hope and encouragement to all quadriplegics. The Superman films, in which he switched so comprehensively from the dull persona of the reporter Clark Kent into the caped costume of the Man of Steel, are a lasting reminder of his athletic grace.
Superman, 1978.
Director: Richard Donner.
Starring: Christopher Reeve, Marlon Brando, Gene Hackman.

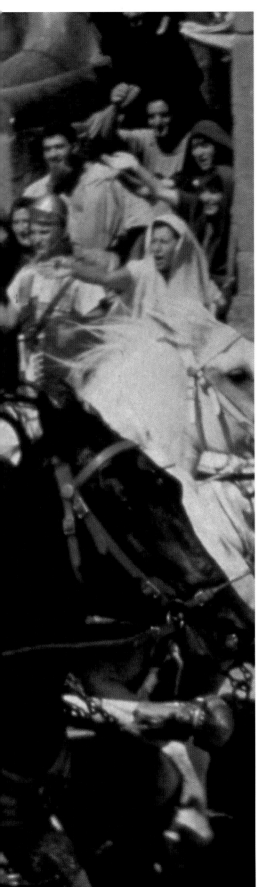

A Match for Messala

◀ The climax of the three-and-a-half hour superlative epic is the 20-minute chariot-race sequence. In a huge arena, the Jewish prince Ben-Hur (Charlton Heston) takes on and ultimately defeats his treacherous childhood friend Messala (Stephen Boyd), who becomes a Roman persecutor. The set took a year to build and covered an 18-acre site, allegedly the largest ever built for a movie. Eight thousand extras filled the stands. The shooting ratio of 65mm film used was also a record, 263 feet to every foot used in the final cut. Heston and Boyd learned the skills of chariot-driving from the former world rodeo champion and most famous of all Hollywood stuntmen, Yakima Canutt.
Ben-Hur, 1959.
Director: William Wyler.
Starring: Charlton Heston, Jack Hawkins, Steven Boyd.

Racing for Life

▲ The silent film epic was not the first time that the nineteenth-century Lew Wallace novel had been filmed. There was a one-reel version in 1907 starring William S. Hart. In the twenties epic, with Ramon Novarro as Ben-Hur and Francis X. Bushman as Messala, the chariot race was originally to have been shot in Rome, but problems arose, including the death of a stuntman, and the set was abandoned. The sequence was finally shot on MGM's Culver City backlot. There were no human fatalities, but a number of horses were killed. Not surprisingly, it remains one of the most thrilling sequences in silent movie history.
Ben-Hur, 1926.
Director: Fred Niblo.
Starring: Ramon Novarro, Francis X. Bushman, May McAvoy.

Road Warrior

▼ Not much notice was taken of this film's initial release, even though the distributors thoughtfully redubbed the Australian accents into American. When a sequel, The Road Warrior, appeared two years later, the original film was looked at anew. The performance in the title role by Mel Gibson, who had emigrated from the United States to Australia at the age of twelve, propelled him into international stardom. Playing a former cop in a bleak near-future in which gasoline has become scarce and precious, he decides to take to the baking desert highways to exact revenge on the bikers who have murdered his wife and child. Mad Max exerted a potent appeal, especially to those who feared the future.
Mad Max, 1979.
Director: George Miller.
Starring: Mel Gibson, Joanne Samuel, Hugh Keays-Byrne.

Captain America and Billy

▶ The script of this film perfectly fits the sour-note finish to the liberating sixties and had been hawked around Hollywood before Columbia decided to offer modest backing. Dennis Hopper (Billy) had been about to give up movies, Peter Fonda (Wyatt, the self-styled Captain America) had his career at a standstill, and Jack Nicholson (George) was, in spite of a string of low-budget Roger Corman films, almost an unknown. Essentially it is a story about doped-up bikers who ride across the face of America seeking a freedom that doesn't exist. Along the way to New Orleans, they encounter hostility and violence from the self-righteous who are affronted by their absurd motorcycles, long hair, and unconventional clothes. What then caught the zeitgeist now seems like a curious artifact of a distant past.
Easy Rider, 1969.
Director: Dennis Hopper.
Starring: Peter Fonda, Dennis Hopper, Jack Nicholson, Karen Black.

Hold the Chicken

◀ For anyone who has endured surly restaurant service, the moment when Jack Nicholson loses his patience strikes powerful resonances. All he wants is wheat toast, but the waitress insists that she can allow no substitutions. Eventually he orders a chicken salad on toast, then tells her to hold the chicken — between her knees. "You see this sign," she snarls. "You see this sign," he says, trashing the table setting. He plays the scion of a music-loving middle-class family who has fled to a blue-collar job in the California oilfields and is making his way north with his uneducated girlfriend (Karen Black), having learned that his father is dying at the family home on an island in Puget Sound. His dilemma, and the cause of his pain, is that whatever world he inhabits he is a misfit.
Five Easy Pieces, 1970.
Director: Bob Rafelson.
Starring: Jack Nicholson, Karen Black, Susan Anspach.

Five Easy Pieces 1970

Fast Eddie Makes a Break

▲ Paul Newman became a superstar on the strength of his performance as Fast Eddie Felson, denizen of the poolrooms, who takes on Minnesota Fats (Jackie Gleason), the toughest player in America, trampling on the psyche of others in the process. The real-life legend of the pool tables, Willie Mosconi, coached them both and doubled in close-ups of intricate play. Newman had a fixation that his best films began with the letter H, hence "Hud", "Harper", and "Hombre". In 1986 he brought Fast Eddie back in The Color of Money, winning an Oscar.

The Hustler, 1961.
Director: Robert Rossen.
Starring: Paul Newman, Jackie Gleason, Piper Laurie, George C. Scott.

Brute Strength

▶ Martin Scorsese chose to shoot this film, based on the rise and fall of the middleweight champion Jake LaMotta, in black and white, echoing such fight films of the 1940s as Champion, The Set-Up, and Body and Soul. Brilliant editing by Thelma Schoonmaker gives the ring encounters a graphic realism seldom encountered in a dramatic feature. A phenomenal performance was given by Robert De Niro, who not only learned to box convincingly but added 50 pounds of real bodyweight to represent LaMotta in decline. An intense portrait of triumph and failure, it was a seminal American movie of the 1980s.

Raging Bull, 1980.
Director: Martin Scorsese.
Starring: Robert De Niro, Cathy Moriarty, Joe Pesci.

Bang, You're Dead

◀ Sensitive audience members suffered seizures when the bandit in Edwin S. Porter's pioneering narrative film, with its 14 exciting scenes taking almost 12 minutes to unfold, turned his gun on them. We can laugh now, but it has to be remembered that not long before the sight of train rushing toward the camera or heavy waves breaking on a shore would have had them cowering and ducking. Porter's thriller told a coherent crime story in a western setting, although in truth the filmmakers journeyed no farther west than the badlands of New Jersey to find a convenient stretch of railroad track.
The Great Train Robbery, 1903.
Director: Edwin S. Porter.

The Man with No Name

▲ With serape and cigarillo, Clint Eastwood cuts a menacing figure in the first and most celebrated of the spaghetti westerns, so-called on account of their Italian provenance, although the Mexican border settings were recreated in the south of Spain. This is a remake of the Kurosawa film Yojimbo, in which a Japanese village hires a samurai to settle two warring factions. Eastwood's character, who rides into the troubled town from nowhere and vanishes as mysteriously at the end, has no past and is ambiguous, a mercenary who never enters into moral arguments. The film elevated him to iconic status and also propelled Ennio Morricone into the front rank of film composers.
A Fistful of Dollars, 1964.
Director: Sergio Leone.
Starring: Clint Eastwood, Marianne Koch, Gian Maria Volonté.

Despair in Death Valley

▶ In the bizarre end sequence of von Stroheim's
film, Gibson Gowland murders his former friend
Jean Hersholt to take a bag of gold. Too late, he
realizes that he is handcuffed to a dead man and
in the scorching heat of Death Valley the gold is
of no use to him. He can only wait to die.
Erich von Stroheim tried to film Frank Norris's
novel McTeague in its entirety, producing a
prodigious work 42 reels in length. Irving Thalberg
removed it from him and had it cut to a mere 10.
The cut material was probably destroyed, but what
remains is still a masterpiece of silent cinema.
Greed, 1924.
Director: Erich von Stroheim.
Starring: Gibson Gowland, ZaSu Pitts,
Jean Hersholt, Chester Conklin.

Geronimo

▲ The Indians are attacking the coach as it speeds across the floor of Monument Valley on the Utah-Arizona border. One of the reins has fallen and if it is not recovered the coach will slow to a halt. The Ringo Kid (John Wayne) jumps from one pair of horses to the next until he can reach and spur the lead. The stunt was actually performed by Yakima Canutt, who also had a role as a cavalry scout. Ford's masterly western helped to revive the genre and catapulted the 31-year-old John Wayne (left, with Louise Platt), who had been in movies for nearly ten years, into stardom. It was also the first time Ford had used the spectacular buttes of Monument Valley as a backdrop, but he would return there many times.
Stagecoach, 1939.
Director: John Ford.
Starring: Claire Trevor, John Wayne, John Carradine, Thomas Mitchell.

Do Not Forsake Me

▶ On the morning of his marriage, Gary Cooper, the marshal of Hadleyville, learns that a vicious killer he sent to jail has been released and is arriving on the noon train to kill him; meanwhile his accomplices are waiting at the depot. The marshal is isolated, with none of the townsfolk willing to help. Even his bride appears to desert him. He can only do his duty. Carl Foreman's screenplay has veiled references to the plight of those who, like him, were blighted by the House Un-American Activities Committee. After being blacklisted for his refusal to name names of Communist sympathizers, he went into exile in England, where he pursued a distinguished career.
High Noon, 1952.
Director: Fred Zinnemann.
Starring: Gary Cooper, Grace Kelly,
Thomas Mitchell, Katy Jurado.

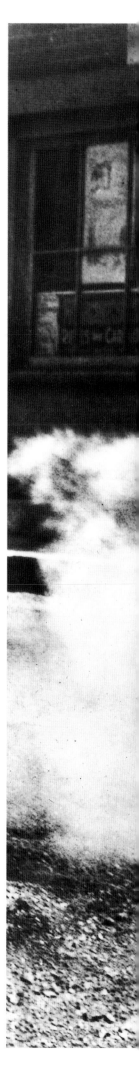

High Noon 1952

The Last Run

◀ The picaresque adventures of the American bank robbers Butch (Paul Newman) and Sundance (Robert Redford) end with this freeze frame as they run from cover to face a fusillade from the rifles of the Bolivian army. Butch's last words as they are cornered are: "For a moment there I thought we were in trouble." Based on the exploits of real life Yanqui banditos, and wittily scripted by William Goldman, George Roy Hill's film sparked a cycle of buddy movies, and worse, irrelevant song interludes, in this case Burt Bacharach's Raindrops Keep Falling on My Head.
Butch Cassidy and the Sundance Kid, 1969.
Director: George Roy Hill.
Starring: Paul Newman, Robert Redford, Katharine Ross.

Butch Cassidy and the Sundance Kid 1969

A Cause Worth Fighting For

▶James Stewart as Jefferson Smith, an idealistic neophyte senator, confronts his former idol, the distinguished Senator Joseph Paine (Claude Rains), whose hands are soiled with graft. Frank Capra's populist film, with its careful recreation of District of Columbia landmarks, was denounced by politicos and the Washington press corps on its first screening, which took place in the Hall of the Daughters of the American Revolution, with cries that such corruption was unthinkable and that the film would be a bad advertisement for America overseas. Fortunately, the New York critics were positive and the moviegoing public even more so. Throughout the world its positive message was recognized.

Mr. Smith Goes to Washington, 1939.
Director: Frank Capra.
Starring: James Stewart, Jean Arthur,
Claude Rains, Edward Arnold.

Stupid Is as Stupid Does

▼Forrest Gump (Tom Hanks) is caught short in the White House, to President John F. Kennedy's amusement, some clever technical trickery suggesting that he was resurrected to play the scene. Forrest's low IQ never handicaps him as he makes a point of ignoring inconvenient information, a luxury the more intellectually gifted populace are required to forsake. He has, like a twentieth-century Candide, the knack of being in the right place at the right time in a hilarious progression through recent American history, embracing peace marches, Elvis, Vietnam, Watergate, and Apple computers.

Forrest Gump, 1994.
Director: Robert Zemeckis.
Starring: Tom Hanks, Gary Sinise, Robin Wright,
Sally Field.

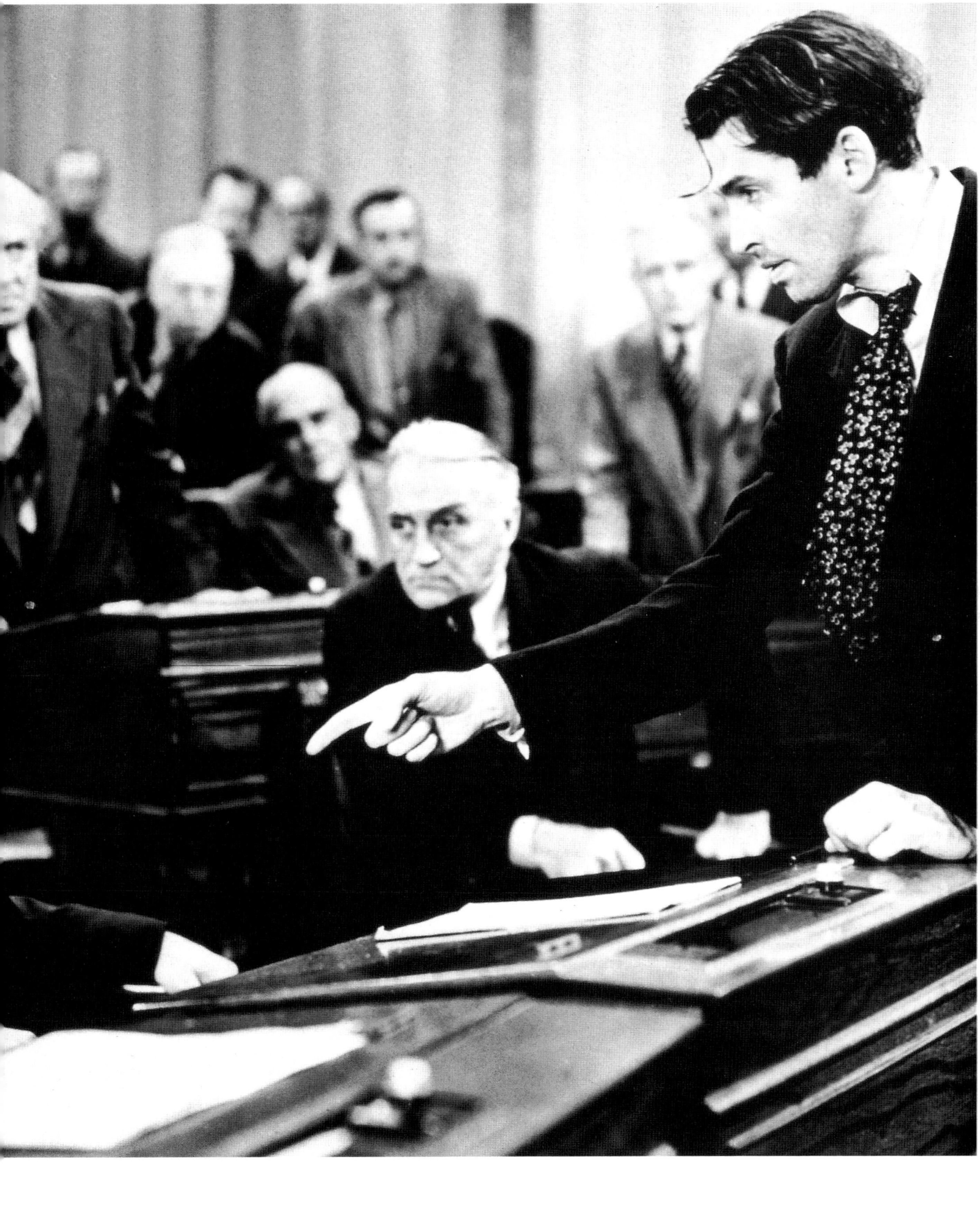

Mr. Smith Goes to Washington 1939

Not a Drinker, a Drunk

▲ Ray Milland, a New York writer fighting his block, is shamed when his girlfriend (Jane Wyman) discovers a bottle hidden on a line dangling from his window. Milland, usually typecast in light romantic comedies, was uneasy at taking on the role of chronic alcoholic, but he was convinced when he realized that the team of Charles Brackett and Billy Wilder had never had a bomb.
The scene in which he walks along Third Avenue attempting to pawn his typewriter was shot quickly with concealed cameras, and two women who had spotted the unshaven star and knew Milland's wife rang her as well-wishers to report that he was on a drinking jag in New York City. The liquor industry tried to stop the film, to no avail. It won several Oscars: for best picture, director, actor, and screenplay.
The Lost Weekend, 1945.
Director: Billy Wilder.
Starring: Ray Milland, Jane Wyman, Philip Terry, Howard da Silva.

Where's the Rest of Me?

▶ If nothing else, this steamily melodramatic turn-of-the-century saga of small-town life from a best seller by Henry Bellaman will be remembered for the moment when Ronald Reagan, as the local playboy, wakes up after a railroad accident to discover that both of his legs have been amputated by a vindictive doctor. "Where's the rest of me?" he says to Ann Sheridan, the girl from the wrong side of the tracks. He always regarded it as the acme of his movie achievement, and he became a star as a consequence of this role. Later he even used the line as the title of his autobiography.
Kings Row, 1942.
Director: Sam Wood.
Starring: Ann Sheridan, Robert Cummings, Ronald Reagan, Betty Field.

A Man Obsessed

◀ Orson Welles, already an enfant terrible of the stage and radio, saw making movies as akin to playing with a gigantic toy train set and overturned accepted rules to create the most innovative of all American films. His media tycoon, Charles Foster Kane, endures hubris as he runs in the senatorial race. The film is a quest to discover the truth about the man, who dies alone, a shattered snow globe offering a clue to the enigma. The sensitivities of the real-life William Randolph Hearst were acute. He instituted a lifelong, vicious vendetta against Welles on the grounds that there could be only one newspaper mogul who could fill a vast estate with treasures gathered from around the globe, and that was himself.
Citizen Kane, 1941.
Director: Orson Welles.
Starring: Orson Welles, Joseph Cotten, Dorothy Comingore, Everett Sloane.

A Smile and
Perhaps a Tear

▲ Memories of childhood in London's fetid slums were not all that distant when Chaplin made his first feature. In this story, he finds a baby boy dumped by a single mother (Edna Purviance) and raises the child to help him with his trade, repairing broken windows. It has a Dickensian touch, especially when the mother, later a wealthy singer, takes the boy away from his broken-hearted surrogate father. Little Jackie Coogan was the son of a vaudeville comedian and had a magical rapport with Chaplin. Late in life, Coogan achieved fresh fame as television's Uncle Fester in The Addams Family.
The Kid, 1921.
Director: Charles Chaplin.
Starring: Charles Chaplin, Jackie Coogan, Edna Purviance.

The Kid 1921

Tears and More Tears

▲ Life in postwar Rome is hard. A father (Lamberto Maggiorani) can work only if he has his own bicycle on which to pedal around the city pasting up billboards. The bike is stolen, and all weekend he and his small son (Enzo Staiola) search the streets in growing despair. The combination of Cesare Zavattini's screenplay and Vittorio De Sica's direction produces a poignant threnody on the theme of poverty and intense compassion for the human spirit. What makes this jewel of Italian neorealism especially remarkable is the unforced chemistry between father and son, neither of whom were played by professional actors. A masterpiece.
The Bicycle Thief, 1948.
Director: Vittorio De Sica.
Starring: Lamberto Maggiorani, Enzo Staiola, Lianella Carell.

Truth Is a Matter of Opinion

▼ A bandit (Toshiro Mifune) rapes a nobleman's wife (Machiko Kyo) in Kurosawa's influential film that established Japanese cinema internationally after it was shown at the Venice film festival. The crime is seen from four perspectives, those of the participants and a witness, each of them offering a different interpretation of events. Which one of the conflicting accounts is the truth? The stunning message of the film is that absolute truth is a fallacy and that all interpretations are flawed by the individual's capacity to believe what he or she wants to believe. Therefore all trials depending on the evidence of witnesses are flawed. *Rashomon, 1950.*
Director: Akira Kurosawa.
Starring: Toshiro Mifune. Machiko Kyo, Masayuki Mori, Takashi Shimura.

Cain and Abel

◄ James Dean, twin son of a Salinas lettuce grower in this adaptation of John Steinbeck's novel, is devastated when his father (Raymond Massey) rejects the money he offers to overcome his father's financial ruin. The old man thinks it has come from a tainted source, the whorehouse earnings of the boys' real mother, who is a madam in Monterey. Dean's performance as the neurotic, vulnerable, self-destructive brother contrasted so with that of his stable, diligent, and sensible sibling (Richard Davalos) that his elevation to mega-stardom was automatic.
East of Eden, 1955.
Director: Elia Kazan.
Starring: Julie Harris, James Dean, Raymond Massey, Richard Davalos.

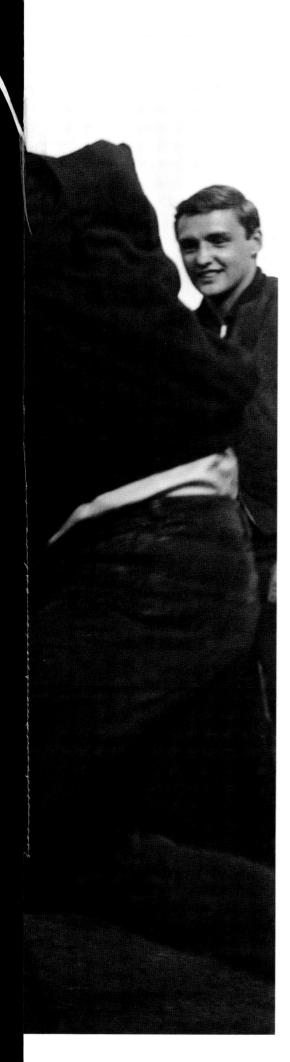

Crazy Mixed-up Kids

◀ The knife fight between James Dean and his high-school challenger, Corey Allen, is resumed later as a chicken run in which both boys drive hot rods to a cliff edge, leaping from them at the last second. One of them fails to get out in time. Two factors ensured the film's success. One was the notion that middle-class children from well-heeled families could be as delinquent as under-privileged slum kids if they were not loved enough by their parents. The other was Dean himself, who was killed driving his Porsche on a Californian highway just as the film was released.
Rebel Without a Cause, 1955.
Director: Nicolas Ray.
Starring: James Dean, Natalie Wood, Sal Mineo, Jim Backus.

In the Heat of the Night 1967

They Call Me Mister Tibbs

▲ Sidney Poitier, well-dressed and carrying money, is automatically arrested in Mississippi as a murder suspect because he is black, but the redneck sheriff (Rod Steiger) finds to his embarrassment that this Virgil Tibbs is a super-intelligent, well-educated detective from Philadelphia visiting his folks. The murder victim's wealthy widow insists that he stay to handle the investigation, and Steiger is forced to work with him in a subordinate role, overcoming his instinctive prejudices. What makes the relationship so satisfying is that both men begin to respect each other's qualities; even if they are never going to be bosom buddies, they part with a sense of understanding.
In the Heat of the Night, 1967.
Director: Norman Jewison.
Starring: Sidney Poitier, Rod Steiger, Warren Oates.

We'll Meet Again

▶ Slim Pickens, an aircraft commander determined that his nuclear bomb should reach its target, manually releases it from a jammed mechanism and rides it to the ground like a bronco as Vera Lynn swells on the soundtrack. The horrific yet farcical concluding moment from Kubrick's black comedy on a doomsday theme ends the best Cold War apocalyptic satire of the sixties, distinguished by Peter Sellers's triple performances as the American president, a British air force officer, and the Dr. Strangelove of the title, a sinister German scientist in a wheelchair whose mechanical arm involuntarily extends itself in Hitlerian salutes.
Dr. Strangelove or: How I Learned to Stop Worrying and Love the Bomb, 1964.
Director: Stanley Kubrick.
Starring: Peter Sellers, George C. Scott, Sterling Hayden, Keenan Wynn.

Whale of a Time

◀ Gregory Peck, as Captain Ahab, obsessed with the whale that tore his leg from him, combs the seas until he finds it, eventually meeting his doom as he becomes entangled in the harpoon ropes of the mortally wounded creature. Herman Melville's novel was carefully filmed using a new color process to replicate the steely look of nineteenth-century engravings, recreating authentic-looking New England nautical communities. Three huge mechanical whales were constructed, two of which broke loose. They were routinely sighted for some time afterward by real whale watchers.
Moby Dick, 1956.
Director: John Huston.
Starring: Gregory Peck, Richard Basehart, Leo Genn, Orson Welles.

Doomed to Die

▲ The ordered life of an aging Japanese government official is suddenly overturned when he learns that he has terminal cancer. Suddenly, as he contemplates dying alone, the shallowness of his existence becomes horribly apparent. He withdraws his money and for the first time goes on the town, to the bemusement of his adult son. There is eventual fulfillment. Against the forces of the bureaucracy that he has upheld, he pushes through a children's playground project. There is a marvelous moment when the dying man, aware of his accomplishment, sits humming on a swing in the completed playground as the wintry snow descends.
Ikiru, 1952.
Director: Akira Kurosawa.
Starring: Takashi Shimura, Nobeo Kaneko, Kyoko Seki.

Dance of Death

◄ The final moments of Bergman's potent film, in which a medieval knight (Max von Sydow), returned from the Crusades, searches for the meaning of existence, were shot at speed at the end of a day to take advantage of a sudden miraculous light. It was done so hastily, in fact, that members of the crew donned the costumes and became the silhouetted figures, the real actors having already left the set. Although the stylized film evokes fierce arguments, its reputation has diminished alongside the director's later work, and its detractors regard it as overly pretentious.
The Seventh Seal, 1957.
Director: Ingmar Bergman.
Starring: Max von Sydow, Gunnar Björnstrand, Bibi Andersson.

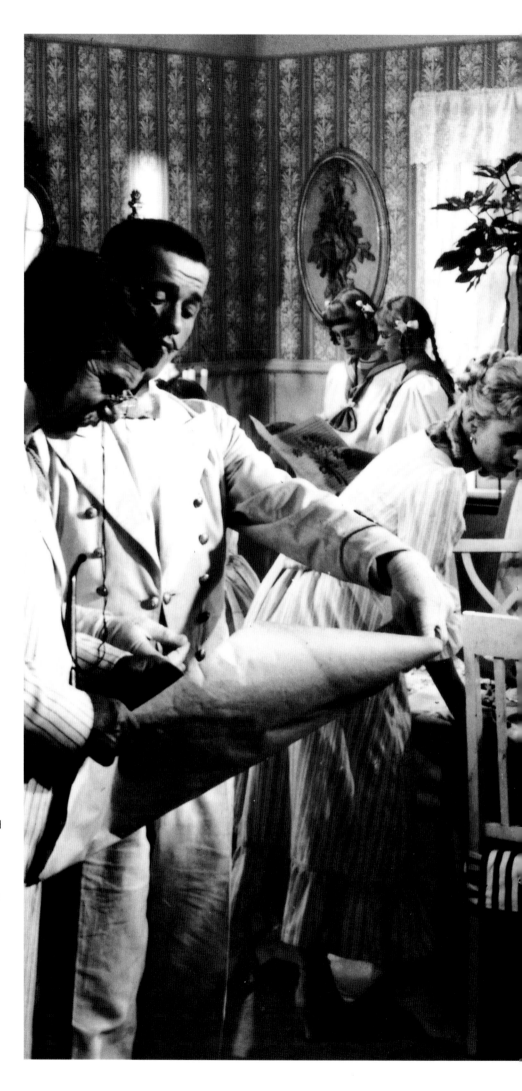

Eavesdropping on the Past

▶ Victor Sjöström, as a elderly professor on his way to be honored at his old university, visits his old family home and recalls his childhood, watching as an unseen presence. The intermingling of past and present in flashback had already been tried in 1950 in an earlier Swedish film, Alf Sjöberg's fine adaptation of Strindberg's Miss Julie, but Bergman honed and refined the device in his elegiac, fondly remembered work. The 78-year-old Sjöström had been Sweden's top film director in silent days and lived in Hollywood from 1923 to 1930, where, as Victor Seastrom, he directed Lillian Gish in The Scarlet Letter and The Wind, and Garbo in The Divine Woman.

Wild Strawberries, 1957.
Director: Ingmar Bergman.
Starring: Victor Sjöström, Bibi Andersson,
Ingrid Thulin, Gunnar Björnstrand.

Index

Picture credits

Every effort has been made to trace the copyright of the photographs used in this publication.
If inadvertent errors have been made, we apologize and ask the copyright holders to contact the producer so they can be rectified.
2–3: Wark Producing Corporation (MOMA).
6–7: Brazil-20th Century-Fox (Courtesy The Ronald Grant Archive).
8: Top, Horizon-Columbia (Courtesy Kobal); Bottom, Riama-Pathé (Courtesy Kobal).
9: Shamley-Paramount (Courtesy Kobal).
10–11: Warner Bros (Courtesy Kobal).
12: RKO (Adelman Collection).
13: Paramount (Adelman Collection).
14–15: MGM (Courtesy Kobal).
15: MGM (Moviestore Collection).
16: MGM (Adelman Collection).
17: MGM (Adelman Collection).
18: 20th Century-Fox (Moviestore Collection).
19: MGM (Courtesy Kobal).
20: 20th Century Fox (Adelman Collection).
21: 20th Century Fox (Adelman Collection).
22: Mirisch, Seven Arts-UA, (Arrow/Pictorial Press).
22–23: Mirisch, Seven Arts-UA, (Pictorial Press.)
24: Warner Bros (Moviestore Collection).
25: MGM (Moviestore Collection).
26–27: Epoch, Museum of Modern Art (MOMA).
28–29: Mosfilm (Moviestore Collection).
30: Cinédis (MOMA).
31: Horizon-Columbia, Columbia Pictures (Courtesy Kobal).
32–33: Horizon-Columbia, Columbia Pictures (Adrian Turner).
34–35: Mirisch-UA (Adelman Collection).
35: Mirisch-UA (Joel Finler).

36: Omni Zoetrope-UA (Adelman Collection).
36–37: 20th Century-Fox (Adelman Collection).
38: Two Cities-Eagle Lion (Courtesy Kobal).
38–39: 20th Century Fox, Paramount (Moviestore Collection).
40–41: Warner Bros (Adelman Collection).
42–43: Left, MGM; Center, Charles K Feldman-Warner Bros; Right, Rollins & Joffe-UA; (all Adelman Collection).
44–45: Samuel Goldwyn-UA (Adelman Collection).
45: MGM (Moviestore Collection).
46–47: MGM (MOMA).
48–49: Selznick-MGM (Pictorial Press).
49: Selznick-MGM (Photofest).
50–51: Warner Bros (Adelman Collection).
52–53: 20th Century-Fox (Adelman Collection).
54: 20th Century-Fox (Adelman Collection).
54–55: Warner Bros (MOMA).
56: Warner Bros (Adelman Collection/Memory Shop).
57: RKO (BFI Films).
58: Romulus-British Lion, UA (Adelman Collection).
58–59: Cineguild (BFI Films).
60–61: Films du Carosse, SEDIF (MOMA).
61: de Beauregard-SNC (MOMA).
62–63: Columbia (Adelman Collection).
64–65: Transcona-Warner Bros (Adelman Collection).
66–67: 20th Century-Fox (BFI Films).
67: Columbia (Joel Finler).
68–69: Embassy, Lawrence Turman-UA (Courtesy Kobal).
70–71: Paris, Five (Adelman Collection).
71: PEA-UA (Courtesy Kobal).
72: Lightstorm, 20th Century Fox, Paramount (Pictorial Press).

72–73: MGM (MOMA).
74–75: Ufa, Paramount (Courtesy Kobal).
75: ABC, Allied Artists (Pictorial Press).
76–77: Paramount (Moviestore Collection).
78–79: Left, Columbia (Moviestore Collection); Center, Riama-Pathé (Courtesy Kobal); Right, Eon-UA (Moviestore Collection).
80: 20th Century-Fox (Howell Conant).
81: Albatros (Courtesy Kobal).
82: MGM (Adelman Collection).
83: Le Studio Canal +, Carolco, TriStar (Moviestore Collection).
84: Top, Warner Bros, (Adelman Collection); Bottom, Howard Hughes-UA (Moviestore Collection).
85: Top, Long Road-Paramount (Adelman Collection); Bottom, A Band Apart, Jersey, Miramax (Adelman Collection).
86: Nero (Moviestore Collection).
87: London, Selznick-British Lion (MOMA).
88–89: Warner Bros (MOMA).
90–91: Warner Bros (Moviestore Collection).
92–93: Malpaso-Warner Bros (MOMA).
94: Tatira, Hiller-Warner Bros (Joel Finler).
94–95: Paramount (Adelman Collection).
96–97: UIP, MGM-UA, Pathé (Moviestore Collection).
98: D'Antoni-20th Century-Fox (Adelman Collection).
99: Hitchcock-Paramount (Adelman Collection).
100–101: MGM (Adelman Collection).
Page 102 Shamley-Paramount (Courtesy Kobal).
103: Shamley-Paramount (Courtesy of Academy of Motion Picture Arts and Sciences/Margaret Herrick Library–Saul Bass Collection).

104: Hoya-Warner Bros (Moviestore Collection).
105: Hawk-Warner Bros (Adelman Collection).
106–107: Orion (Pictorial Press).
107: Columbia (Adelman Collection).
108–109: Hal Roach-Pathé (Joel Finler).
110–111: Chaplin-UA (Adelman Collection).
112–113: Keaton-UA (Adelman Collection).
114–115: MGM (Courtesy Kobal).
116–117: Chaplin-UA (Adelman Collection).
118–119: Ealing-GFD (Courtesy Kobal).
120: RKO (Courtesy Kobal).
121: Mirisch-UA, United Artists (Courtesy Kobal).
122: Woodfall, Holly-British Lion, Bryanston (Moviestore Collection).
123: Star, Prominent, MGM-UA (Adelman Collection).
124–125: Decla Bioscop (MOMA).
125: Ufa (Moviestore Collection).
126–127: Universal (Joel Finler).
127: Universal (Courtesy Kobal).
128–129: RKO (Moviestore Collection).
130: Columbia-EMI (Moviestore Collection).
130–131: MGM (Courtesy Kobal).
132: Buñuel and Dali (Adelman Collection).
132–133: Warner Bros (Adelman Collection).
134: Lucasfilm-20th Century-Fox (Moviestore Collection).
134–135: Lucasfilm-Paramount (Courtesy Kobal).
136–137: Universal (Adelman Collection).
137: Star Film (Courtesy Kobal).
138–139: Dovemead, IMF, Warner Bros (Courtesy Kobal).
139: Gordon, Silver, 20th Century Fox (Moviestore Collection).
140–141: MGM (Moviestore Collection).

141: MGM (Pictorial Press).
142: Mad Max Pty (Adelman Collection).
142–143: Pando-Columbia (Adelman Collection).
144–145: BBS-Columbia (Adelman Collection).
146: 20th Century-Fox (Moviestore Collection).
Page 147: Robert Chartoff & Irwin Winkler-UA (Adelman Collection).
148–149: Edison (MOMA).
149: Jolly, 20th Century-Fox (Adelman Collection).
150–151: MGM (MOMA).
152–153: Walter Wanger-UA (Moviestore Collection).
154: Stanley Kramer-UA (MOMA).
154–155: Stanley Kramer-UA (Joel Finler).
156–157: 20th Century-Fox (Adelman Collection).
158: Paramount, (Courtesy Kobal).
158–159: Columbia (Moviestore Collection).
160: Paramount (MOMA).
160–161: Warner Bros (Courtesy Kobal).
162–163: RKO (Adelman Collection).
163: RKO (Courtesy Kobal).
164: Chaplin-First National (Adelman Collection).
165: PDS, ENIC (BFI Films).
166–167: Warner Bros (Moviestore Collection).
167: Daiei (Adelman Collection).
168–169: Warner Bros (Adelman Collection).
169: Mirisch-UA (Moviestore Collection).
170–171: Moulin-Warner Bros (Adelman Collection).
171: Hawk-Columbia (Adelman Collection).
172–173: Svensk Filmindustri (MOMA).
173: Toho (MOMA).
174–175: Svensk Filmindustri (MOMA).